Change is rough.

I thought that maybe I had to face my loss of Matt to find my music again. I prepared myself for that, for turning sadness and grief into self-righteous anger so that I could move on.

I did not expect to look deep within and find a serious need to change.

And even now…you'd think an internal change would be just that: internal. But it's affecting everything and everyone around me.

Figures.

First String

The String Serial
Part One

Andrea Ring

Originally published in 2016 by Square Gorilla Press. For information, visit http://www.squaregorilla.com.

ISBN 978-0692729861

Dedication

To my mother, Laurinda Claus, who is the only person on the planet who thinks I'm funny.

Acknowledgements

Thank you Michael and Hannah for taking the scary leap into book cover creation. I'm blessed to have you both.

Chapter 1

I sit sullenly in Dr. Steinburg's office, staring at my painted toenails. Va-Va-Va-Voom, the red polish is called. I hate the color, and know it only makes my white skin look whiter, but Matt loves it when my nails are red.

Loved it.

"Why do you think your mother is so worried about you?" Dr. Steinburg asks.

I sigh. "No big mystery. My husband left me, and she thinks I'm depressed."

"Are you depressed?"

"Not pill-popping depressed," I say. "I get up, go to work, pay my bills."

"So you don't think you need to be here."

I sigh again. "You've been treating my mother for fifteen years, so you know how screwed up my childhood was, and that's reason enough for me to need to be here. But if fifteen years weren't enough to cure her, I'm not sure you're that good at what you do."

"Try me," he says. "Your mother is paying for the sessions. What have you got to lose?"

I finally raise my eyes to his. "I'm sure she's told you everything. What do you want to know?"

"Tell me about your marriage."

I shift in the overstuffed chair. "Big question. Matt was my childhood sweetheart, literally. I loved him and that was it. We got married two days after graduation, and now, ten years later, here we are."

"Here you are, where?" he asks.

"Here. Divorced. He left me for a teaching assistant in his department at the university. That's it."

"Were there signs that he was the unfaithful type?"

I shrug. "Not really. I never...I thought..."

Dr. Steinburg looks at me patiently. He makes no move to speak. And tears gather in my eyes for no good reason.

"He was my rock," I say softly. "I had all this chaos at home...cokehead dad, doormat mom, arguments and brawls and weeping spells and days where my mother refused to get out of bed...and there was Matt. He rescued me. And then he dumped me."

"Tell me about Matt."

"He's...kind. Generally, I mean, mostly. Nice. Polite. He has a quiet voice, so different from my dad. He never yells. He can get mad, but it's a quiet mad. He'll look like he's about to burst, and then he'll meet my eyes, and it's like the anger just washes away. He was so respectful of what I needed. Always."

"Except for the fact that he left you for someone else."

I laugh. "Yeah, well, there's that."

"He must have had some flaws," Dr. Steinburg says.

I think about it. "He wasn't that great at communicating," I say. "I mean, I always got the feeling that he was holding back and not sharing every thought in his head."

"Why do you think that was?" he asks. "Because, obviously, he was hiding a great deal."

I shrug again. "I don't know."

Dr. Steinburg leans back in his chair. "You know, often, we choose what we know. You knew an abusive, drug-addicted father, and it would have been easy for you to choose the same for a husband, because that is your known. But you went the opposite direction. You chose a quiet, polite man. One who refused to even yell when he was mad so that he wouldn't upset you."

I nod.

"There's something very noble about that."

I crack a smile. "Thank you."

"But…it didn't work. Something was off. Do you think he tried too hard not to upset you?"

I blink. "What do you mean?"

"Maybe, sometimes, he needed to yell. But perhaps he felt stifled because he knew he couldn't yell at you."

I press my lips together. "So you think he left because he couldn't be himself?"

"I don't know without talking to Matt. But, let's say he did yell. What would you have done?"

"He yelled," I say. "Twice. He was allowed to yell."

"Twice. In how many years?"

"Seventeen," I say. I force myself not to add the extra two months and twelve days.

"And how did you react?" he asks.

"How does anyone react when their husband yells?"

I get the stare again.

"I cried," I finally say. "He always said he hated to see me cry."

Dr. Steinburg hands me a tissue, and I take it and dab at my eyes.

"Let's leave that for now," he says. "So Matt was your first boyfriend?"

I nod.

"First kiss, first lover, first everything?"

I nod again.

"Have you dated anyone since?"

I laugh. "It's only been six months. I can't just turn off seventeen years of loving someone and date someone else."

He nods. "How long do you think you need to wait?"

"I'm not waiting for anything," I say. "I just…"

Patient nod. Patient stare.

"I don't know what I want," I finally admit. "I had Matt. That's all I thought I'd ever have, all I thought I ever wanted."

"What is your idea of the perfect man?"

I picture Matt in my head. "Dark hair, brown eyes, kind voice. Nice."

"Is that a description of Matt?"

I wrinkle my forehead. "Well, why not?"

The sarcasm hangs between us.

"What do you like to do in your spare time?"

"We used to go to baseball games. We had season tickets for the Angels. And we always had people over, you know, for barbecues, so I would cook and entertain. We used to ride our bikes around town."

"Do you still do those things? Now?" he asks.

"No."

"Do you want to do those things?"

I just stare at him.

"Let me offer something," he says. "I think you grew to be an adult only in the context of your relationship with Matt. You were Matt's girlfriend. Matt's wife. And it's a wonderful thing to be in a relationship and care about your role in it, but you didn't take the time to think about who you are as a person. An individual. Who is Hope Russell?"

I laugh nervously. "Do I have to answer that?"

"I don't believe you can answer that," he says. "Not yet. But that's why you're here. I don't think you're depressed. Sure, you're sad, and you have a right to that. Seventeen years out of twenty-eight is a big chunk of your life. You're starting fresh. You have to figure out what you want out of life without Matt in it."

My eyes sting. "I don't know how to do that."

"So here is your assignment," Dr. Steinburg says. "I want you to explore your interests. Take a class, or join a club, find something that interests you and try it out. It doesn't matter whether or not it sticks. You just need to do something for you."

"You think that will help me get over the love of my life?"

"It's a start. And the second thing I want you to do is have a wild affair."

My mouth falls open. "You want me to sleep around? When I've been with one man my entire life?"

"I'm not suggesting a one-night stand. I'm saying you need to give yourself permission to try things out. Including men. You've known exactly one, but there are a zillion different men out there, each with the capacity to teach you something about yourself. Every relationship doesn't have to be a lifetime commitment. A relationship can be that, of course, but look at it like shopping for a car. You don't just buy the first car you see. You compare prices, you test-drive them, you ensure they have enough cup holders. There are a lot of great cars out there, but they're not all a great fit for you."

He rises just as the hands of the clock slide to ten minutes 'til three. I take the hint and rise with him.

He smiles. "How about we give it a month? I'll have my receptionist call you to schedule."

I nod. One session a month. My mother's gone cheap, and I can only be grateful.

Chapter 2

My phone rings as I slide into my car.

"Hey, Ma. The session went fine."

"Did he put you on Prozac?"

I roll my eyes. "I'm not depressed. I told you that. He wants me to find a hobby."

"A hobby? He's up to his old tricks. I tried that in 2005."

I smile. "Did it work?"

"I spent $1000 on golf lessons, and all I got were a few calluses for the effort. Honestly, Hope, you need drugs."

"Said no mother to her daughter ever," I say. "I'm hanging up. And he's your therapist. Maybe I should try someone else."

"No!" she says. "No. I trust him. Forget I said anything. Follow his advice. I just...I hate to see you so sad."

My body sags. "I know. Listen, I've gotta run. I'll see you for dinner tomorrow."

"Don't be late! See you then. Bye!"

"Bye, Ma."

I throw the phone into my purse and start my car. My mother.

She means well. Truly. Finally. I give her credit for it, but sometimes...she's a bit much. Like she's making up for years of bad parenting. Which she is.

We're at a good place now. She's attentive to me, and takes care of herself, and we can actually talk. I've let go of my resentment for the years she spent placating my dad and putting us both in harm's way. I barely remember the fights anymore. I can watch two actors arguing on TV, as long as it's a comedy, and not feel like I need to run.

Matt always hated that. He'd put a movie on, the latest thriller or action thing, and he wanted me to watch with him. I tried. But if violence came on, or voices were raised…I didn't even think about it. My feet hit the floor, and my body stood up, and I'd be out of the room.

I pull into a parking space and look up. Without realizing it, I'd driven to the Tustin Town Cinema.

Who is Hope Russell? Dr. Steinburg asked me.

A girl who runs, I think.

I grab my purse and exit the car. Watching a movie isn't exactly a hobby, but it's an activity. Something to do on a Saturday afternoon. And Dr. Steinburg mentioned that—*What do you like to do in your spare time?* I was too embarrassed to say I play Free Cell on my computer or clean the house.

"One ticket, please," I say to the pimply-faced teenager behind the glass.

"Which movie?"

I look up at the marquee. There's the latest Disney flick, some slasher crap, a Nicholas Sparks romantic tragedy…

"*Navy SEALs to the Rescue*," I say. "Is that one violent?"

"The SEALs don't tap dance, as far as I know," he says.

"Right. Great. I'll take it."

Chapter 3

The theater is mostly empty when I enter. I take the seat nearest the exit and take a deep breath.

The first time a gun is fired, I literally jump in my seat. And the blood...my stomach rolls.

I rush out of the theater and into the open, gulping fresh air and trying to calm my heart.

"You okay?"

I startle and turn.

"I'm sorry, hey, I'm really sorry," a guy says. "I didn't mean to scare you. I saw you run out. Are you okay?"

I shake my head. "Fine. I'm fine. I just don't like those kinds of films."

He smiles, and it's kind of lopsided. "What kinds of films?"

"The bloody kind."

"Then why'd you see it?"

I smile back. "A personal challenge of sorts. I'm really fine."

He's staring at me a little too hard. Not in a creepy way, but it's...uncomfortable.

"Well, I appreciate the concern," I say. "I should get going."

I turn to go, but he stops me with a hand on my arm, which he quickly snatches away. "Wait. I'm Sam. I just...you were gonna watch the whole movie, right? So you don't have anywhere you need to be."

I raise an eyebrow at him.

"Maybe I can buy you a cup of coffee."

"A cup of coffee."

He grins. "Yeah. And a muffin. Or maybe a scone. You look like you could be a scone girl."

I laugh. "What does a scone girl look like?"

"Pretty," he says. "Beautiful brown eyes. Soft, hesitant smile. Red toe nails." He looks pointedly at my feet.

I wiggle my toes. "I'm divorced," I say, and then I cringe. Why the hell would I say that?

He laughs. "Scone girls are awkward, too. In a charming kind of way."

I blow out a breath. "I'm an idiot. And woefully out of practice at this."

He holds out his hand. "Like I said, I'm Sam. I can call you Scone Girl, but I'm sure your name is sexier."

I shake his hand. "I'm Hope."

He grins. "I knew it."

Chapter 4

"I'm a grad student at UC Irvine," Sam says. "History. You?"

I sip my chai latte. It has a weird taste, but whatever. Sam asked me what I wanted, and when I couldn't decide, he decided for me.

"I have my bachelor's in English," I say. "I'm a copyeditor for Nikon. I write their technical manuals."

"Do you write anything besides technical?" he asks.

"Novels, you mean?" I say, and he nods. "No. I keep a journal, but I've never felt that creative."

Sam leans forward. "You said you were divorced, right?"

I pick at the lid of my coffee. "Yeah."

"All great artists are fueled by their personal angst," he says. "Maybe you should try to tap into that."

I cringe again. "I'm sorry. Is it that obvious? My angst?"

He smiles. "It was the first thing you told me about yourself. I'm guessing it's on your mind. How long has it been?"

"Six months."

"And I'm guessing you haven't dated anyone since?"

I laugh. "I haven't dated anyone else, ever. I'm not just out of practice—I've had no practice."

Sam takes a sip of his coffee. "You need to get laid."

"What?" I say, laughing in discomfort. "That's a little presumptuous."

He laughs, too. "Just an observation. You need to move on."

I wave a hand. "What about you? You're single, I'm guessing."

"No, but my girlfriend's cool with it. She lets me pick up sexy strangers at the movie theater."

My eyes widen. "Oh. I, uh…I don't think—"

Sam laughs again. "I'm kidding, Hope. I'm single. Totally single."

I blow out a breath. "Shit. I thought you were serious. Wait. You think I'm sexy?"

He grins. "You could be."

I roll my eyes and we both laugh.

"So history," I say. "Why history?"

"Mostly 'cause it doesn't feel like work," he says. "I get to read and write fantastic real-life stories." He points to a pile of papers sitting on the table between us. "Although teaching history is a different animal. The way my students write about it is painful."

"You're implying you're a poor teacher," I say.

He holds his hands up. "The semester just started. I can't be blamed yet. I'm actually an awesome teacher."

I sit back. "Teach me something."

Sam meets my gaze, and a soft smile creeps to his lips. "I think you need extra attention. Private lessons. Definitely private."

He has crazy blue eyes, the kind that are so light they look otherworldly. But his lashes are dark, his eyebrows strong. His hair is a bit too long, like he has better things to do than get a haircut. He's not my type, I don't think, but he's not unattractive. In fact, I love his smile. It's boyish, charming and roguish and endearing all at the same time.

"I don't know if I'm ready for that," I say. "I'm flattered, I mean, I haven't even looked for this, but I just don't know."

"Stand up," he says.

I pop to my feet. And then I feel completely foolish. Why did I simply follow his command?

He stands up next to me and takes the coffee from my hand. He sets it on the table.

"Don't think about it," he says. "Just go with it."

"With what?"

He leans into me. Too late, I realize what's happening, and I find myself frozen in place. Sam's lips meet mine, and I'm as stiff as a statue.

He pulls back an inch, and his breath fans my face. "You're not trying. Look at my eyes. Listen to my voice. We're just two people, making a connection."

My hands are shaking. I clench them into fists, and I stare into his eyes. He smells…not bad, just different. When I kissed…when I kiss someone, I have an expectation of the scents, the feels, the sights. This is just strange.

Sam places his lips on mine again. I take a deep breath, and his scent fills my lungs. I soften my lips and mold to him. His hands come up and cradle my face, and his touch makes my eyes sting. I place my hands on top of his and grip tight.

He shifts his stance, and I feel his hips bump mine. He opens his lips, just a bit, and I open mine. Our tongues meet on a sigh, and suddenly his lips crush against me, and I tilt my head, and we're glued together.

"Wow," he breathes against my mouth. "Better."

I grin. "You think?"

He steps back shaking his head. "Damn, I'm good. I knew you were sexy."

We take our seats, and Sam pulls out his phone.

"Can I have your number?"

I hesitate, and he grabs my hand across the table.

"I have class in thirty minutes, or I'd stay," he says. "Let me take you out."

"You want to take me on a date?"

He smiles. "If you'll let me."

I don't know what to say. I have no idea what I want. And I just kissed a stranger. In public.

"There's a concert tonight, at the Galaxy. A bunch of us are going. How about that? Totally casual, big group, no pressure. We can just hang out."

"What kind of music?"

He looks at me with that goofy smile. "I'll try not to be offended that the kind of music might actually sway your decision. It's an 80s cover band. If you're feeling bold, you can dress up."

I take out my phone and hand it to him to exchange numbers. "Scone girls can be bold. When we try."

Chapter 5

There's a long line of people outside the Galaxy when I arrive. I almost turn around and go back to my car—I mean, what am I doing? This is like a Punk'd episode. Get the meek little girl to show up and watch her thrash around helplessly, looking for the cute boy who lured her here.

But as I hesitate, I see Sam emerge from the crowd and jog over to me. His hair is plastered up in a Flock of Seagulls wave, and he's wearing a worn Duran Duran t-shirt. He gives me a hug before I can move.

"So glad you made it!" he says. "You look great."

I smile at him. My best friend Martika helped. I didn't want to go too out there, but she convinced me to wear the blue eye shadow, the side ponytail, and the resurrected Guess jean skirt I saved six months to buy when I was twelve. "Thanks for asking me. Love the hair."

Sam grins. "Come on. Looks like they're letting everyone in." He takes my hand and leads me over to the line.

"Do we have good seats?" I ask.

"No seats. Standing room only. This way I get to see you dance."

Oh good Lord.

"Hey everyone," Sam says as we hit the line. "This is Hope. Hope, this is Dave, Jack,

Mandy, Sarah, Owen…and that's Sophie." Everyone says hi, and I try to smile back. Dave reaches into a paper bag at his feet and pulls out two beers. He hands one to each of us.

"Hurry," Dave says. "You have just enough time to pound one before we go in."

Sam clinks his beer to mine. "Bottoms up."

I look at the beer. It's the same IPA that's stocked in my fridge at home, waiting for Matt to come drink it.

Sam chugs, and I think, *What the hell?* I put the bottle to my lips and drink.

I finish before Sam does, and his friends cheer. Sam raises an eyebrow at me, and I blush.

"I don't drink that often," I say. "Just trying to be bold."

He laughs. We throw our bottles away as the line moves forward, and suddenly we're inside.

Music blares. Lights flash. Sam squeezes my hand and leans into my ear. "Awesome, isn't it?"

If you like this kind of thing, I guess. It's overwhelming, like I'm inside a disco ball. But is it awesome? I don't know how to feel about it. I've never been to an actual concert…not since I was a child.

We settle in the middle of the crowd, and the band takes the stage. It's so loud I can barely hear myself think, let alone talk, but Sam keeps hold of my hand, and somehow, we're connected without even speaking.

Thirty minutes ago, I was embarrassed at the thought of dancing. But when you're in a crowd of people, all with the same purpose, it's impossible not to go along. I find myself jumping and cheering and singing, and Sam holds me from behind and grinds his hips into mine, and I lean back against him and rest my head on his chest, and he leans into my neck and kisses me softly.

I've never thought of 80s music as particularly sexy, but something about this night has my body humming. And I haven't felt that since high school.

When the concert ends, I don't know what to expect. Maybe a goodnight kiss, hopefully a request for another date. Just to see. I mean, I don't even know Sam, but it couldn't hurt to see.

He walks me to my car and then takes me in his arms. He gives me a soul-quaking kiss.

"Come home with me," he breathes into my ear.

I pull back. "To your house?"

He nods. "It'll be good, Hope," he says. "So fucking good."

I bite my lip. "I'll go, but I can't promise. I mean, I don't know how far I can promise to go."

He grins. "Got it. I came here with my friends. Can you drive?"

I nod. "Tell me the way."

Chapter 6

Sam has a one-bedroom townhouse near the university. It's fairly neat and the furniture looks new. I don't know what I expected, but it wasn't this.

"How old are you?" I ask him as he throws his keys on the kitchen counter.

"Thirty," he says. "I know it seems a little old for a grad student, but it took me a while to figure out what I wanted to do. I spent six years as a studio musician."

"Really?" I say. "What instrument?"

"Guitar."

My heart beats faster.

"Do you miss it?"

He grabs two beers from the fridge, pops the tops, and hands one to me. "I still play. But the musician's life is rough. I prefer a steady job."

"Would you play something for me?"

He leans on the counter and grins. "You're gonna make me work at seducing you, huh?"

I take a sip of beer. "Seeing as I'm not fully committed to being seduced...yes."

"I thought the hair would do it."

I laugh. "Oh, the hair is sexy. It's definitely not that."

"I thought the dancing would do it," he says. "Aren't all women turned on when they dance?"

I smile. "I've heard that. But for me…honestly, Sam, I have no idea."

"He really screwed you up, didn't he?"

I frown. "It wasn't him. It's just that he's the only experience I have. We had this life, and this relationship, and I just went with it."

Sam sips his beer. "What did he do to turn you on?"

"Nothing," I say automatically, and then I laugh. "I mean, we were at the point where he didn't have to do anything. The love was just there."

He looks at me, and it almost looks like pity. Like my relationship with Matt was pitiful.

Maybe it was.

"Have you felt anything, even a little twinge, all night?" he asks.

I look away. "That's embarrassing."

"Why?"

"I can't talk about it," I say. "I'm not used to talking about it."

"But that's a good thing," he says. "You need to do things completely differently. You need to try new things. And I can help."

I shake my head as he comes to stand before me. "I don't know why you're even bothering," I say. "I sound pathetic to my own ears. This is way too much trouble for you."

"The payoff is worth it," he says, brushing my hair from my cheek.

"What's the payoff?" I ask.

He shrugs. "In the long run, who knows. But for tonight, it's this." And he pulls my body tight against his, and I can feel his erection, firm, against my hip.

I gulp.

He sets my beer on the counter and presses into me again. "If I do something that feels wrong, just tell me. I want this to be all about you."

"Why?" I say. "Why would you do this? You don't even know me."

"That's how I get turned on," he says, nuzzling his mouth against my neck. "If it's good for you, it'll be amazing for me."

He slowly strips the clothes from my body. I pull his shirt over his head and throw it across the room. When he reaches behind me to unsnap my bra, I push him away.

"I want to explore you first," I say.

He grins and leads me to the bedroom. He climbs on the bed and leans back against a mound of pillows.

"Whatever the lady wants," he says.

I can't believe this moment. I'm here, in my underwear, staring at a half-naked man who is not Matt.

Matt was all athletic muscle. Years of baseball and soccer and weightlifting had bulked him up and sculpted him. That body is the only one I know.

Sam's body is completely different. He's lean, like a cat. His chest isn't as hairy. His stomach is flat, and his hipbones protrude, but he doesn't have the ab definition I'm used to.

"I like your body," I say aloud, and when Sam laughs, I mentally slap myself.

"Good."

I kneel next to him on the bed and run my hands over his chest. He groans as my hands roam lower, skimming his hipbones.

"You could take off your bra," he says with a grin. "I mean, if you want."

"I'm working up to it," I say.

My hands move to his jeans. He lifts his hips, and I work the buttons loose. I slide the jeans down his long legs and gulp again.

He's wearing boxer briefs, totally sexy. Matt preferred...ugh. I growl. Why the hell am I thinking about Matt now?

Sam. Sam is the man in front of me. Sam is the one who wants me. Sam.

He kicks off his jeans and puts his hands around the waistband of his underwear. "You ready for this?"

I nod.

The underwear comes off. And I'm staring at a cock so thick I don't think I can get my hand around it.

"Wow," I say. "Holy shit."

Sam laughs. "That's the best reaction I've ever gotten."

"I…wow."

I stare at it. It twitches. I reach a hand out and slide it down the length of him.

"Christ, you're killing me," he says.

"In a good way?"

He smiles and closes his eyes. "The fucking best way."

I've always liked giving head. There's something powerful about it, about being in control, about giving pleasure rather than taking it.

But oral sex on the first date? What kind of girl does that make me?

Who is Hope Russell?

Maybe I am a slut, and I just never had the chance to express it.

I grip his cock tight and bend forward. But Sam pulls away from me and pushes me gently backward.

"I said this was all about you," he breathes into my mouth. He kisses me hard, and I relax under him.

Before I know it, my underwear is off, and Sam is kissing my stomach. I fight not to laugh, but my stomach muscles are shaking.

"Does that tickle?" he asks, licking my belly button.

"A bit."

He lifts his head. "Then laugh. If that's what you're feeling, do it."

"Laughing isn't sexy," I say.

He shakes his head. "Laughing is the sexiest thing you can do."

"But I don't want to hurt your feelings."

"You can't," he says. "I know this is taking a lot of trust for you, and I want you to feel that from me. Whatever you do, whatever noise you make, however you touch me, it's all good. We're doing the most intimate thing two people can do. Let's have fun with it."

"I'm having fun," I say. "I hope you know that."

He laughs. "I think you're still stuck in your head, and that's okay. But by the end of the night, I'm gonna get you out of it or die trying."

"And how are you going to do that?"

Sam gives me that goofy grin. Then he slides down until his head is between my thighs, and he buries his mouth against me.

"Oh, God," I breathe, and a million thoughts rush through my head. I fight to banish them. I tell myself to be in this moment.

I feel Sam's five o'clock shadow rubbing against my thighs. I feel his thumbs pull me apart. I feel his tongue as he licks down the very center of me in long, firm swipes, flicking my clit on every upstroke.

My inner right thigh twitches. It's never done that before.

"Tell me what you like," he says, his breath cool against my moist flesh. "Tell me when I hit the spot."

I can't speak. I dig my fingers into the sheets and grip them tight.

He concentrates on my clit with his tongue, and puts two fingers inside me. I cry out as they sink deep.

I feel my orgasm building. My thighs shake, and my fingers clench, and my head thrashes.

He notices that I'm close, I think. He backs off, moving his thumb to caress my clit while his mouth moves lower. And lower.

"What are you doing?" I say.

"Just go with it."

"But I—"

Sam suddenly lifts his head. He moves his hand to his mouth and pulls out a tiny torn piece of toilet paper.

My mouth falls open in horror. "Oh my God." I sit up and cover my breasts, and it feels like I might throw up.

He laughs. "Hope, calm down. It's fine."

"Fine? It's not fine! I can't believe…I'm gonna go die now." I move to get off the bed, but he puts his hands on my thighs and keeps me there.

"You can't be embarrassed," he says with a grin, and I stuff my face in the pillow. "Well, okay, you can, but you don't have to be. It's no big deal."

"Yes, it is," I mumble into the pillow.

"Laugh about it," he says. "I am."

I lift my head and bash his chest with the pillow. "That's for laughing at me."

"Come on," he says. "Give me one little giggle. I know you want to."

He makes me smile. I try to fight it, but I can't. My lips split, and laughter bubbles out of my throat, and in my effort to suppress it, I snort.

Sam laughs out loud, and I join him. He tackles me back against the pillows, and we laugh into each other's mouths.

Until we're kissing. My arms are around him, and I'm feeling every slope, every plane, every dip of his body, and he sneakily slides back down between my legs and licks me with pointed tongue.

"Sam," I breathe, and he goes lower, pushing my legs up higher until my ass is totally exposed, and I dig my heels into the mattress and he licks me where I never even contemplated being licked.

My clit tingles. And he's not even touching it.

"God," I say. "I've never…I've never felt that."

He puts a finger inside me, and then moves it to that lower entrance. "You've never done this?"

I shake my head, and he smiles.

"Just relax. Let all your muscles relax. You'll like it."

He licks my clit again and probes with his finger. I can tell I'm too wound up, too tight, but I can't make myself relax. Just the tip of his finger manages to go in, but as he licks, and my orgasm builds once again, my muscles unclench of their own free will.

His finger slides in. All the way in.

Oh. My. God.

And my orgasm hits, and my hips buck, and Sam concentrates on my clit, and pumps his finger, until every last drop of pleasure is squeezed out, and my body spasms, and his finger withdraws, and I didn't realize how filled up I felt until it's gone.

He lifts his head and I look down at him. He's smiling, but he has blood on his lips.

"You're hurt!" I say, sitting up and leaning toward him. I put a finger to the blood and show him. "You're bleeding!"

He licks at the blood and grabs a tissue from the nightstand. "Bit my tongue. But it was worth it."

"Did I do that?" I say.

He smiles. "When you came. I didn't expect it. My fault."

"It's my fault," I say. "I'm so sorry."

"No apologies. You came harder than anyone I've ever been with. I'm taking it as a compliment."

I blush. "You were…incredible."

"It was the ass, wasn't it?" he says, running a hand down my leg. "You liked it."

"I didn't expect to," I say. "I can't believe I let you do that."

"I can do it again."

I smile. "I think it's your turn."

"You don't have to," he says. "I mean, you can, if you want, but you don't have to."

"I want to."

We trade places.

I give as good as I got.

Chapter 7

I've already met Sam's friends, but the concert didn't really count. I didn't get to have a conversation with any of them, and I doubt I could tell you what any of them looks like. I was pretty much in awe of the music and only focused on Sam.

But for date number two, Sam's invited me to pizza and a ball game at his place. Baseball I can do. It's one of the few topics I know inside and out.

I'm the first to arrive, and I think Sam planned it that way. He greets me with a bone-crushing hug around my neck first, and then a slow, wet kiss. But both are awkward because my hands are wrapped in oven mitts, and I'm holding a hot crockpot.

"Let me set this down," I say against his lips, and he laughs.

"Sorry. Got a little carried away. I see you and I have to touch you."

I blush and hide it by running to the kitchen. I set the crockpot down and slide off my mitts.

"Queso," I say. "My special recipe. I just have to run back to my car and get the chips."

"Grab a beer and relax," he says, moving to the door. "I'll get them."

He's out the door before I can blink. Wow. Matt never offered to help bring groceries in. Even when I returned from Costco, and he watched me lugging in a case of water, ten pounds of laundry detergent, and box after box...he just sat there, his eyes glued to the television.

Then again, I never asked for help.

Sam comes back in. "Did you get a beer?"

I shake my head. Frankly, I forgot about it.

He moves to the fridge and hands me a bottle. "Do you think it's poor etiquette to dive into the queso before the guests arrive?"

I smile. "I'm a guest, and I've arrived."

"Excellent point." He tears open the bag of chips and lifts the lid of the crockpot. He digs a chip in and shoves the whole thing into his mouth. His eyes close, and his lips lift in a smile as he chews. "Man. You're a queso goddess."

I laugh. "That's the best reaction I've ever gotten."

He slits open one eye and grins. "Eat a chip so I can kiss you without worrying about my queso breath."

I smile, take a chip, and scoop up a big bite. Before I even finish chewing, he's on me, pressing his entire body against mine, and backing me up against the fridge. His hands roam, and my body grows warm.

"I could marry you for your queso, you know that?"

"Man cannot live on queso alone."

"This man could."

I laugh.

The door opens, and two people spill in. Sam smiles at me, pecks my cheek, and moves to his guests.

"Dave," he says, slapping the guy on the back. "And the lovely Sarah."

"I burned the wings," Sarah says, "but we brought them anyway. Maybe someone wants to torture themselves."

Dave smiles. "I told her we could just order them along with the pizza, but she was feeling domestic."

"You make that sound like a dirty word," Sarah says. "*Domestic.*"

"You guys remember Hope?" Sam says.

They both turn to me. "Hey, Hope," Sarah says. "Nice to see you again."

"You, too," I say. "You know, the wings don't look that bad."

Dave snorts. "Are they supposed to be black?"

"I personally don't mind that," I say, "but for those that do, they can just peel the skin off."

Sarah looks triumphant. "I told you we shouldn't just dump them."

I laugh. "Are you learning to cook?"

"I don't know that I'm actually learning anything," she says, "but I'm trying."

"May I?" I gesture to the wings.

"They're your taste buds," Dave says, and Sarah pokes him in the stomach.

I grab a wing and take a bite. Yes, the burnt char taste is bitter, but I can taste the sauce, too, and it has good flavor. "They're good," I say. "Did you make the sauce?"

She nods. "I wasted two pounds of butter."

"You cooked them with the sauce?"

She nods again.

"The sauce burns," I say. "That's the problem. Cook your wings first, then coat them with the sauce."

"You cook a lot?" she asks.

"Yeah. I love feeding people."

"Dave's birthday is next week," she says to me quietly. "Would you help me? I want to bake him a cake."

I smile. "Love to."

We exchange numbers and set up a time. Sam and Dave have moved the queso and chips to the coffee table, and they're totally silent, shoving chips into their mouths. On the TV, the teams are announced and the first batter steps up.

"Do you like baseball?" I ask Sarah.

She shrugs. "I've gotten used to it since Dave and I moved in together. It's a good excuse to hang out with friends."

"I used to go to almost every Angels home game," I say. "It wasn't really my thing, either, but my ex loved it."

"When'd you guys split?" she asks.

"About seven months ago. Sam's the first guy I've dated since."

"Sam's a good guy," she says. "I met him in college, and we hit it off right away. Not in a sexual way, just as friends. He's had a tough time finding someone."

"Why's that?"

She smiles. "He tends to go for the chemistry and ignores everything else. Chemistry is great, I mean, you've gotta have some chemistry...but it doesn't last. There has to be more, you know?"

I nod. "Are you saying he's mostly dated bimbos?"

Sarah laughs. "I try not to be mean about other women, but...yes. Dear God, were they all beauties with no brains."

"Then why the hell is he dating me?"

Sarah looks at me, startled, I think, by the honesty in my question. "You've got both," she says. "Maybe he hasn't figured out how much substance you have yet."

I laugh. "Thanks for that. But seriously…I'm not that special-looking, and I'm not saying they're recruiting me to MENSA or anything, but…is he just looking to get laid?"

She takes my hand and squeezes. "I've totally screwed up by telling you all that. Ignore me. Sam is a good guy. He deserves someone like you, and I think he's serious. He really wanted us to hang out with you today. That says a lot."

I nod. "Enough second-guessing then. What do you do?"

"First grade teacher," she says. "You?"

"Technical writer," I say. "First grade? You must be a saint."

She smiles. "I love it. I absolutely love my job. It takes some patience, but that's my gift. I can't cook, but man, I can tie shoelaces and wipe snotty noses and sing 'Happy Birthday' all day long."

I shake my head. "I've never even been around kids. I'd have no idea how to do any of that. Well, I can tie a shoelace. And I can sing. But I'm totally jealous."

"You've never been around kids?"

"Nope. Only child, very little extended family…even my ex's family hadn't gotten around to having kids yet."

"You should come to my class and help out one day. I mean, if you want." She laughs. "It's an experience."

I grin. "I just might have to try that."

Sarah moves to the bag of groceries they brought and pulls out a wine cooler. "You want one?"

I hold up my beer. "I'm good for the moment."

She shakes her head. "I've tried, but I just can't drink beer."

"Hey," Sam calls. "If you guys want queso, you better get over here. We're demolishing it."

Sarah and I move to the couch and sit with the guys.

"I don't know why they started Billings," Sam says, referring to the pitcher. "The guy's older than dirt."

"He has the best ERA on the team," Dave says.

"But that's only because he's played so few games," I say. "Hernandez is slightly higher, at 2.4, I think, but he's started at least fifty more times. I think they're saving his arm. Oh, and two of Oakland's starters are lefties. Billings does better than Hernandez against lefties."

I dip a chip. Everyone's gone quiet. I look up, and Dave and Sam are staring at me open-mouthed.

"I didn't know you knew that much about baseball," Sam says.

I smile. "Now you do."

"I don't know anyone who knows that much about baseball," Dave says, shaking his head. "Not that's female, anyway."

Sarah slaps his arm. "Why does it surprise you that a woman knows about baseball?"

"Do you know anything about baseball?" he asks her.

"You know I don't."

"Proves my point. I know I've shacked up with a feminist, but you can't ignore reality. Men are more into sports. Accept it."

Sarah scowls, but she doesn't argue.

Pizza arrives, along with Owen and Mandy. Sarah and Mandy eventually wander to the kitchen, and I feel out of place. I mean, I could watch the game, I'm happy to watch it, but I don't have to. I could hang out with the girls. Maybe I should be hanging out with the girls.

I move to get up, but Sam stills me with a hand on my thigh. "I was just gonna get another beer," I say. "You want one?"

"I'll get it," he says, bounding to his feet.

I sit back and a commercial comes on. Dave scrapes the bottom of the crockpot with a bunch of chip crumbs.

"How'd you get into baseball?" he asks.

"My ex," I say.

He shakes his head. "I need to meet this guy and learn his tricks. I can't get Sarah to sit down and watch a whole game."

"The trick is to give her an incentive," I say. "The game is not an incentive. But if you rubbed her feet while you watched the game, I bet she'd stay."

"I usually eat during a game," he says. "Rubbing feet and eating is kind of gross. Give me something else."

"Pick a body part that she likes to have rubbed," I say.

Dave laughs. "I know a few of those."

I laugh, too. "Or maybe when the commercials come on, turn your attention to her. If she's doing something for you, do something for her. Like a throw a load of laundry in the washer."

He stares at me like I've just spoken a foreign language. "Did your ex actually do that?"

I smile. "Always."

"I love Sam, but dude, that guy had skills."

I laugh again. "We were together since the sixth grade. I had years to train him."

"Sixth grade…shit. I can't even imagine that. One woman for literally my entire life? That takes some balls."

"Balls?"

"Yeah," he says. "Marriage is the biggest commitment you'll ever make, right? The biggest decision? And to have confidence that your junior-high self knew what the fuck you wanted out of life? Damn. I wish I trusted myself that much."

I sigh. "Well, since we're not together anymore, I guess you could say we didn't know what the fuck we wanted."

Dave gives me a sympathetic smile. "His loss is Sam's gain."

"You think so?"

He nods. "And Sarah's, too. I'm actually thinking about doing the laundry."

We both laugh.

Chapter 8

Dr. Steinburg eyes me as we take our seats. "You look different," he says.

"I met someone," I say. "I left here that Saturday, and I couldn't think of anything I wanted to do. A hobby, I mean. I had no idea what I was going to do, but I ended up going to a movie. I don't know if my mom ever told you, but I can't watch violent movies, or family drama, anything where people hurt each other. I've never been able to watch that stuff. So I thought I might try it."

Dr. Steinburg chuckles. "I wasn't expecting you to torture yourself, Hope. Facing our fears and our phobias can be a good thing, but sometimes it's an unnecessary thing. How'd it go?"

"Not too well," I say. "I saw that Navy SEALs flick, and I lasted about twenty minutes. But I met a guy outside the theater. We had coffee and then we went to a concert. He's…nice."

"Just that one date?"

I shake my head. "We've been out six times this month. We're getting to know each other."

"I think that's great," he says. "Have you been intimate?"

"A bit," I say. "We haven't actually…you know, but we've done some things."

"And how do you feel about that?"

I twist my hands in my lap. "It was weird. It is weird. If I think about it too hard…it feels like a betrayal."

"To whom?"

I shrug. "Me, I guess. Being only with Matt was part of who I was. I was proud of that. It felt loyal and virtuous. But I gave that part of myself away."

"You had to," he says. "If you want to find love again, you had to give it up. And there's nothing wrong with that. You can still be loyal and virtuous."

I nod. "I know. I just…I think working myself up to actual sex is going to be tough."

"Why is that?"

"It means that Matt and I are really over."

Dr. Steinburg's eyes soften. "You and Matt are over, Hope. He's moved on. You deserve to do the same."

"I'm trying."

He smiles. "Tell me about this new man. What do you have in common?"

"Well…he's a musician."

Dr. Steinburg raises an eyebrow.

"I know. I know what you're going to say. But that's what he used to do. Now, he's a history PhD candidate. He wants to teach and write."

"Have you told him who you are?"

I purse my lips. "That's not who am I."

"It's a part of you," Dr. Steinburg says. "You can't deny that."

I don't say anything.

"You are the daughter of one of the most highly regarded guitar players of all time," he says. "You should embrace that."

"I'm the daughter of a drug addict who beat my mother, beat on me, and died of a drug overdose on the toilet. That's how I remember it."

"Do you still play? Your mother has told me how nimble your fingers are."

I shrug. "I haven't lately."

"I don't bring this up to dredge up old memories or hurt you," he says. "But sometimes we need a new perspective. You don't have to hold your father up as a hero, because we both know that would be a lie. But he was gifted. He passed that gift to you. If that is the only good thing we can take from him, then I think you should take it."

"What does this have to do with anything?" I grumble.

"You have a new man you are getting to know, but you haven't let him in. You've only known him a month, so of course, you haven't shared everything, but it's going to start weighing on you. You don't have to share the bad. Share the good."

"What do you mean?"

"Correct me if I'm wrong, but…music is your life."

"My mother talks too much."

Dr. Steinburg smiles. "It's just something to think about. This new man will never know you unless you share the important things."

Chapter 9

I think about my session on the drive home. What does Sam really know about me?

Nothing. I haven't even been able to tell him that I prefer Corona to that hoppy IPA crap, or that I take my coffee black, no chai. He knows my father is dead, but I haven't shared anything about the circumstances.

I haven't picked up a guitar since Matt left. I used to play every day, five times a day, but now...my music's wrapped up in Matt. All my memories, of sitting outside classrooms, waiting for a mother who was chronically late to pick me up, strumming away on my guitar...of Matt sitting with me, waiting, often walking me home...of playing for him before bedtime, after dinner, around the bonfire at the beach...

I get home and go to the spare bedroom. I take my bass off its stand.

There are certain songs I just can't play yet. And that's fine. As Sam likes to say, I need to do things differently.

I choose a Duran Duran song, which reminds of Sam. "Come Undone" has a bass line—it's actually played by the keyboardist, but it sounds like a bass line—so I play it.

An hour passes before I even realize it. Damn. I missed this.

I put the bass back and take my phone out of my pocket.

"Hello, gorgeous, I was just thinking about you," Sam says when he answers.

I smile. "I know we were gonna have dinner with Dave and Sarah, but would you mind a change of plans?"

"Yes, you can come over and cook naked."

I laugh. "Actually, I thought maybe you could come to my place. I'll cook for you, and…there's something I want to show you."

"I get to see the Scone Girl's house? For real?"

"I think you've earned it."

Sam laughs. "Done. I'll call Dave. What time?"

"Whenever you're ready."

ℴ

Sam arrives at six with a bottle of wine. He gives me a lingering kiss and holds up the bottle.

"I don't know what we're eating. I hope it goes with red."

"Whatever you like," I say, carrying it to the kitchen. Sam follows me, swiveling his head to take in my house.

"Wow. Was your husband rich?"

I shake my head. "Actually…that's part of what I want to show you tonight. I didn't make anything fancy, just lasagna, so we have time while it cooks."

Sam smiles. "Does it involve lace? Or silk?"

I laugh. "No. More like steel and wood."

He pulls me to him. "I knew you were kinky like that."

I laugh and kiss him. Then I take his hand and lead him to the couch. "Stay here."

I go to the spare room and grab two guitars. Then I stand before him.

His eyes go wide. "Is that a Martin?"

I nod. "A 1929 Martin Vintage. They only made 15 of them."

He tears his eyes away from the guitar and looks at me. "I didn't know you knew about guitars."

"I'll get to that. And this is a 1963 Fender Stratocaster. My dad left me these."

He stands. "May I?"

I pass him the Fender.

"This has seen some serious playing. Did your dad play?"

"A bit."

He examines the guitar. "I can't...I almost don't want to play it. It's like you can feel the music just by touching it."

"I always thought that," I say. "Somehow, you can hear the guitar just by looking at it."

Sam lowers himself to the couch and pats the seat next to him. I sit.

"What do you hear, Hope?"

"Russell is my married name," I say. "Did I tell you that?"

He shakes his head.

"My maiden name is...Cruz."

He blinks at me.

"And I play. I mean, you can't be Joe Cruz's daughter and not play. And I should have told you. When we went on that first date, and you told me you were a musician, I should have said something. But I just don't talk about it."

Sam looks at his lap. "Do you still play?"

"Today was the first day I've played since my divorce. I was thinking about you, and I wanted to tell you...but before that, I played every day. Music is a big part of me."

He raises his eyes to mine. "Why not just say that? You know how important music is to me, too."

"That made it even harder," I say. "When I hear people worship him like he's some kind of god…you know how he died, right?"

Sam nods.

"Imagine that. He was a drug addict. And he had a temper. My mom and I had to live with that."

"God," he says. "If I remember right, you're the one who found him, didn't you?"

I nod.

Sam pulls me against him. I'm not sad, exactly, since all I have is bone-deep hatred for the man. I guess I'm more ashamed. And then I'm frustrated, that every person on the planet sees my father as great when only I know the truth.

"Seems like you got the best of him, baby," Sam says into my hair. He kisses my head and pulls back. "Can I hear you play?"

I smile. "What should I play?"

"What do you know?"

"If I've heard it, I can play it."

Sam laughs. "Shit. Okay. Play your favorite song."

"I don't think you'll know it." Sam raises an eyebrow, and I laugh. "Okay. I'll be super impressed if you know it."

He rubs his hands together. "A challenge."

Something hot gleams in his eyes. My body shivers. I pick up the Martin and set it on my lap.

I play the introduction of Depeche Mode's "Stripped." I want to sing along, but that would give the song away.

Sam leans back and closes his eyes.

"It's not meant for guitar, is it?" he asks.

"Keyboard," I say, still strumming.

He opens his eyes. "Depeche Mode."

I stop playing. "I can't believe you know it."

He frowns. "I'm a musician, too."

I blink. "Did I offend you? I didn't mean to."

"No." He gets to his feet and walks to the kitchen.

I set the guitar down and follow him.

"I did. I offended you."

He shakes his head. "Can I get a drink?"

"You want me to open the wine? Or I have Corona."

He laughs. "Corona? Isn't that a little light for you?"

I bristle. "It's what I prefer."

He turns his back on me and sits down on a stool at the island. "Corona's fine."

"What's wrong?" I ask. "What did I do?"

"You're finally opening up," he says, not meeting my eyes. "I just never thought this was what you were hiding."

"I haven't been hiding," I say. "I've just never had to open myself up like this. We've only known each other a month."

"A month where you met my sister, and you heard me play, and you've met my friends…I thought I was okay with all that. With you being…coy. But I guess I'm not."

"What does that mean?"

He laughs. "You like fucking Corona. Every time we've eaten together, have you been holding your nose? Every time we've kissed…have I been doing it wrong?"

"You're blowing this out of proportion," I say. "You knew I didn't open up easily. But I haven't lied. So I prefer Corona. So what?"

"I'm surprised you even drink, with Joe Cruz for a father."

I narrow my eyes at him. "Get out."

"Jesus, Hope, I didn't mean it. Not like that."

"I said, get out."

"Hope—"

"No!" I yell. And the loudness of my own voice startles me, but it also gives me courage. "Do you know what it took for me to invite you here tonight? Nobody knows! Nobody knows the real me. Fuck, I don't even completely know the real me! And you're throwing it in my face!"

Sam scrubs a hand over his face. "I'm sorry."

I sag in place. "Don't be. This is the real you, your real thoughts. I shouldn't...I can't be mad at you for that. I mean, I don't like it, but at least you're being honest."

"I like you, Hope. A lot," he says.

"But not the real me."

"I'm just getting to know the real you," he says. "It's a shock. I have to fit these new pieces into the puzzle."

"Okay," I say. "Call me. I mean, if you want to."

"Call you?" he says. "You think I'm leaving? I'm not. I just need a minute to process."

"Oh."

"I thought we'd finally be having sex tonight."

I stare at him and cross my arms over my chest. "So I get real on you and spill some serious shit, and now I've ruined the mood. Silly me."

"That's not what I meant," he says. "I spent the last month playing songs for you, and even writing songs about you, and now I find this out and hear you play...I feel like an idiot."

"You wrote songs about me?" I say. "Wait. Why do you feel like an idiot?"

"You don't know how good you are, do you?"

"Good at what?"

Sam shoots to his feet. "Are we having the same conversation? The guitar! You're fucking brilliant!"

"I…you only heard me play that one song."

"That's all I took," he says. "It's the most comfortable I've ever seen you. You had this look on your face…I've never seen that look."

"What look?"

"Perfect contentment. Everything's right with the world. You're in love."

I nod. "That's how I feel when I'm playing."

"I want you so bad," he says, and then he takes a deep breath. "Honestly, you don't know the real me, either."

Something cold slithers down my spine. "What do you mean?"

"I've been holding back a lot with you. I didn't want to scare you or push you."

"You mean in the bedroom." I make it a statement and he nods. "So…what have you been holding back?"

"I'm not gonna tell you unless you can handle it," he says. "I'm so turned on right now, I'm afraid that if we start, I won't be able to stop."

"You can't say that and expect me to agree just like that," I say. "What if you want to do something horrible?"

Sam scratches his chin. "What's your definition of horrible?"

"I don't know," I say. "Pain. I don't like pain."

He shakes his head. "I'm not into that."

"Bodily fluids. Other than the usual."

Sam grins. "I have no plans to pee on you."

I blow out a breath. "Thank God."

He moves to me and runs his hands down my arms. "I just want to ravage you. Hard and fast, music blaring, with no time for either of us to think. I want to get lost with you."

I almost ask him why. I mean, yeah, maybe my guitar playing was a turn on, but he saw something in me even before he knew I played. I desperately need to know what it is that he saw.

But I don't ask, because Sam has been so patient with me. This is the first thing he's truly asked for since we met. And I want it, too. I need it. I have to move on.

I lead him to my bedroom and put on some music. Foo Fighters' "Everlong" blares through my radio.

I strip my shirt over my head and unclasp my bra. I slide my skirt to my ankles and press myself against him.

"Is that a yes?" he asks.

"Don't talk," I say. "Just do it."

Chapter 10

There's nothing here but us, Sam and me, and Dave Grohl's perfect acoustic guitar.

Sam sheds his clothes and bends me over the bed. He cups my ass and then rips my thong right off me.

Damn. Those were expensive.

I clench my teeth. *Stop thinking!* He wants me so badly he fucking tore my underwear off! Concentrate on that!

He licks a moist line down my spine. It's kind of gross. I mean, his spit is drying on my back, and it's making me shiver. In a cold way.

He gets to my ass crack, and as his tongue swirls around, I giggle. It tickles. I look over my shoulder, and he gives me a smile.

The smile I love.

He nibbles at my hips. "I want to watch you," he says.

"Watch me what?"

"Play with yourself."

He flips me over and I scoot up closer to the headboard.

"Um."

"Touch yourself, Hope," he says.

I thought we were going to make love. I prepared myself for that. Bu this…this is different.

I tentatively rub my breasts. Sam watches me closely with hungry eyes, and he seems to be enjoying it. Okay. I can do this.

I move my hands lower. Sam grips his cock as my hand slides between my thighs. Now I'm the one watching closely.

Matt and I…we didn't do this. Okay, maybe we tried it once or twice, but it wasn't a part of our regular repertoire. I don't like to be watched. Who the hell knows what kinds of faces I'm making?

"I want to touch you," I say. "Please. Don't make me watch from over here."

He chuckles. "You're embarrassed again."

I nod.

"I've seen you come," he says. "Several times. You know why I want to watch you?"

He's still rubbing his cock. And I can barely concentrate on anything else. "It turns you on."

"Nope. I mean, it does, but I want to see the way you like it. I want to know exactly what to do."

Something in me softens. Sam's always been like this, encouraging me to express myself, to be myself, but in this moment, he doesn't have to. He can just get laid. And he's putting that off for me.

"If I'm gonna do this, I need to be able to see you, too," I say. "All of you. Can you stand up?"

Without comment, Sam crawls off the bed and stands where I have the perfect view.

"Can you come like that?"

He squeezes his cock. "Fuck yeah."

I lean back and close my eyes. The music washes over me, and I let it fill my head, pushing out every nasty thought, every doubt, every bit of insecurity.

I caress my neck with one hand and squeeze one breast with the other. I pinch my nipple, roll it between my fingers, pull on it until I feel that bolt of lightning shoot down between my legs.

My other hand roams over my chest, down my belly, and to my thighs. Mmmm. I lick my lips. I open my eyes and watch Sam stroke his cock in an easy rhythm.

I open my thighs wider and slide one knee up. My fingers find my clit, and I pinch it. I flick it while my other hand flicks my nipple. I lick my lips again and slide one finger deep inside myself. Then two.

I slide them in and out, and my breath comes faster, and I watch Sam's rhythm pick up. His thigh muscles are rock hard. I abandon my breast and move that hand to my clit.

I rub it with two fingers while I pump the others in and out of my pussy. I rub faster, and Sam moves in sync with me, and I moan as my orgasm builds, and Sam moans, too.

And suddenly he's on top of me. His tongue tangles with mine, and he lifts my leg up over his shoulder, and I feel his condom-wrapped cock rubbing on my inner thigh.

"Now," I say into his mouth. "Now. Fuck me now."

He reaches down and guides his cock. I'm so wet that it slides halfway in with one gentle push of his hips.

"Tell me if it's too much," he says. "Tell me—"

"It's not," I say. "More. Give me all of it."

He props himself up with one arm and reaches the other between us. His fingers find my clit, and he rubs me as he sinks his cock deep.

I gasp. It's not painful, exactly, but it is. I've never been stretched like this.

He starts out slow, moving his hips in circles to give me time to adjust. And he keeps working his fingers, sending shivers down to my toes.

"I'm close," I say. "So close. Fuck me, Sam."

He draws out slowly, and then pushes into me hard. My clit throbs.

"Again," I say. "Again."

So he does it again. He takes back my mouth, and sucks on my lip, and I cling to him, my hips meeting his, our tongues entwined, until an orgasm rolls out from the center of me and sets every nerve-ending on fire.

I cry out.

Sam moans into my mouth, and pumps into me harder, and suddenly lifts his head, crying out, too. He collapses against my chest, and I laugh.

He pushes up and looks down at me with a grin. Then he kisses me.

"You're amazing, you know that?" he says.

"I was pretty good, wasn't I?"

We both laugh.

"Did I hurt you?"

"Not even remotely," I say. "I would have said something."

"Would you have?"

"I know I'm not great at expressing myself, but I don't let myself be hurt."

Sam rolls over onto his back and pulls me against his chest. "Is it too soon to say the L-word?"

My heart thumps and I swallow hard. "We agreed to be honest, right? To the best of our ability?"

He nods and turns his head to me. "I think I love you."

I don't know what to say. I like Sam. A lot. I might love him. Maybe. Quite possibly.

"I think I might love you, too," I say.

Sam laughs, and we just cuddle.

Chapter 11

I wake to my body throbbing. In a good way. All is dark, and Sam's spooning me, his hands gently rubbing my breasts, his cock an insistent ache against my ass.

I flip over and take his mouth with mine. Our hands roam, and I move on top of him.

"Condom," he says. "In my jeans pocket."

Thank God he remembered that. That's one mistake I do not want to make when I'm only possibly sorta maybe in love.

I shuffle through the clothes on the floor, trying to find his jeans. But I'm completely blind.

"I need a light," I say. "Shield your eyes."

"No way," he says. "Not when I have the chance to see you naked."

I smile and flip on the light. I find his jeans and fish in the front pockets. "Got it," I say, and when I hold the condom up, Sam's eyes widen.

I look in my hand. It's not a condom. It's a little baggie of white powder.

My hands begin to shake.

"Hope."

"Is this…what is this?"

He hops off the bed and grabs the baggie out of my hands. "It's no big deal. Sometimes I like to party. It's not a regular thing."

I sit on the bed, and Sam kneels at my feet. "I meant what I said. I love you."

"Don't," I say. "Don't do that. I can't. I'm sorry, Sam, but I can't."

"It's not—"

"I don't care!" I scream. "You knew, I told you who I was and what I went through, and you fucked me with a fucking bag of cocaine in your pocket!"

He looks up at me, and his eyes have turned glassy. "I'll stop. I'm not addicted. I'll never touch the stuff again."

"No," I say. "I can't do this. I won't do it. You need to leave."

He climbs to his feet. "Can I call you tomorrow? Maybe you'll feel differently."

"I won't."

I watch him dress, and I follow him out. At the door, he pauses and puts a hand on my cheek.

"I'm sorry," he says.

I nod. "Me, too."

Chapter 12

Dr. Steinburg listens politely while I tell him of my disastrous affair with Sam.

"You should be immensely proud of yourself," he says. "You cared about this man. It would have been easy to give in, but you didn't. You stood up for yourself."

"The shitty part is that he was good for me," I say. "He was a good person. He genuinely cared about my feelings."

"You need to be strong," he says. "The drugs are a deal breaker."

"I know," I say. "I have no intention of getting back with him. It just…I think I'm a different person now. In a good way. He helped me come out of my shell."

"That's what happens when we meet new people, even the bad eggs. We learn about ourselves. We grow. Are you open to another relationship?"

"Actually, I'm itching for one," I say. "It was nice to have someone to talk to and to do with things with. I miss Sam, but it's not an ache like it was with Matt. I think I can try again."

"And what about the hobby? Any movement on that front?"

I smile. "No. But I've picked up my guitar again. Does that count?"

Dr. Steinburg shakes his head. "Something new. Something adventurous. Something you've never tried. How about rock climbing?"

I laugh. "Rock climbing? There's no way. I can't even do a pull-up."

"How about surfing?"

"When I was five, my dad made me watch *Jaws*. It scarred me for life."

He frowns. "I swear, if the man weren't already dead, I'd strangle him."

I grin. "Thanks."

"How about yoga?"

"My mother does yoga. If she found out I was doing it, she'd insist on going with me, and I have no desire to see my mother in yoga pants."

Dr. Steinburg chuckles. "Then give me an idea. Just one."

I sigh. "Fine. I'll go rock climbing."

Chapter 13

I dragged Martika with me, and now I'm regretting it. She's an absolute stud. Four years in the Navy honed her body, and two hours in the gym every day keeps it hard as a rock. I'm fit, but I still have some jiggle. And now I'm standing at the bottom of the wall next to her, and I've agreed to climb first, and all I can think about are the hundred people here, mostly men, who will be watching my ass.

Martika leans into my ear. "Your ass looks great," she says.

I smile at her. She always knows exactly what I'm thinking.

"Just don't fall," she says. "That would be embarrassing."

"Thanks for the pep talk," I say, giving her a jab with my elbow. Martika just grins.

"Any time you're ready," our instructor says.

"So I just...climb up the wall?" I ask. "I mean, that's it?"

Rock-climbing-master-of-the-world Jeremy laughs. "Pretty much."

Martika pushes me forward. I stumble and glare at her. And then I straighten my spine and march to the wall.

I grip two of the handholds, and Jeremy appears at my side.

"Think about what you're doing," he says. "This is physics. If you hold on here, at shoulder height, you won't have the leverage you need to pull yourself up. Try these two, up higher." He physically removes my hands from the grips and places them on two up higher. "Good. Now, go."

I put a toe on one of the lower thingies, and I push myself up. My other leg flails, trying to find a grip.

I hear Martika giggle, but I'm dangling from a wall and have no way to glare at her.

"Here." Jeremy takes my dangling foot and guides it to a grip. "You got it?"

I'm splayed like Gumby. "Now what?"

"Move your hands up one level," he says. "Then move one of your feet up."

I move my left hand up to a higher grip. But to move my right, I have to hang on with my left arm, and it's about as strong as a wet noodle. So I lean into the wall, all my weight on my toes, and throw my right arm up. Luckily, my hand hits a grip, and I cling to it for dear life.

"Great! Now your legs."

Um.

No one told me it would be this awkward. My knees are at right angles to the wall, and my cheek is smooshed. I feel like a fly splattered on a windshield.

"Hey, Martika."

I freeze. I'd know that voice anywhere. What the fuck is Matt doing here?

"Hey, asshole," she says. Ah. That's my bestie. "You can go now."

"Really?" he says. "We've known each other since sixth grade. I know you and Hope are close, and I'm glad she has you, but it takes two to end a marriage."

"Not when one of the people in that marriage is fucking someone else."

"I guess that's it then," he says. "You're not interested in the truth."

And then Jeremy yells, "Come on, Hope! You can do it!"

Christ.

"That's Hope?" Matt says. "On the wall?"

I imagine Martika nodding and thinking to me hard, *Come on, baby. Go. Climb! Show him what you've got!*

So I grit my teeth and move one foot up. Then I push with all my might and boost myself up. Dangly leg manages to find a hold, and I pause, panting.

"Yes!" Jeremy cries. "Again!"

Again. Right.

There are no holds above me. Now I have to go left or right if I want to go up.

There's no way I can let go with my hands. I need a boost from my legs first. So I put an awkward leg out and up about three feet away from me, and now I'm doing the splits. My inner thigh screams at me.

"The purple one!" Jeremy yells.

Purple…purple…I don't see a purple hold, except for the one my splayed leg is on. Maybe that's what he means. So I move my other foot to the same purple hold, and now I'm sideways on the wall, my arms are shaking, and my fingers are getting slippery.

"Help!" I yell.

"Just let go," Jeremy calls. "I've got you."

But there's no way. Something in me won't let go.

"Let go, Hope!" Martika calls. "You can start over."

I want to, I do. I want my feet on solid ground. But my body won't respond.

"Hey. It's okay. I'll catch you."

I look down. Matt is standing just below me, maybe two feet away. I've only climbed eight feet off the ground.

Sigh.

So I let go. I only drop about a foot before Jeremy's expert belaying arrests my fall, but my feet swing down from their sideways perch and clip Matt in the side of the head. He crumples to the ground.

∽

Martika laughs hysterically as we get in the car.

"I got it. I got the whole thing! Holy shit, was that funny."

I pull out of the parking lot, and laughter bubbles in my throat. I don't want to laugh at Matt's misfortune, but it was kind of funny.

"You are not posting that on Facebook," I say.

"Hell, yes, I am," she says. "You have to see the position you were in. I've never seen anything like it. You were Spider Woman."

I drive as she watches the video on her phone. Again. I hear myself scream and a loud thud as my legs hit Matt and he falls.

"So what time tomorrow?" she asks.

"What time for what?"

"Uh, barbecue. Our house. Benny's friends are in town for the reunion. Stop me when it actually clicks..."

"Right. My mom's torturing me with a friendly tennis game at the club. I'll have to go home and shower...say, five o'clock?"

"No later," she says. "Everyone'll be at our house at four. I promised them the human karaoke machine."

"I'm never invited as a guest," I say. "I have to fill in as the fourth in the tennis match, or be a machine. What happened to saying, hey, Hope, come on over, hang out, and have a burger with us?"

She waves a hand. "If I thought you could just come over and hang out and be social, that's exactly what I'd say. But if you don't have a guitar in your hand, you won't speak. I'm helping you."

I sigh. "And Benny's doing the cooking? Do you think that's a good idea?"

She shrugs. "As long as my husband does it, I don't have to."

"Good point. Except that he actually wants to keep his friends, right?"

Martika smiles at me. "You keep an eye on the burgers, and I'll keep the beer flowing. By the end of the night, they'll love us."

Chapter 14

So it's been a year since I picked up a racquet, and I was never that good anyway. But as the result of Dr. Steinburg's Bright Idea of 2002, my mother and I have to spend quality time together every Sunday. In fourteen years of this, I've picked the activity twice. Every other time, I've been left to go along with whatever harebrained scheme my mother managed to think up.

Tennis might not seem that harebrained, but when you consider that it's a mixed doubles match with her latest conquest as her partner, and that conquest's son as mine...yes. Harebrained.

I arrive exactly on time, but the three of them have already warmed up.

"Finally," Mr. Conquest says as I enter the court. "I thought we'd have to start without you."

I pointedly look at my watch. "My mother said three. It's one minute to."

"Did I?" my mother says, coming over and kissing my cheek. "I'm sure I said two-thirty."

I bite my tongue and hold out my hand. "Nice to meet you. I'm Hope."

Mr. Conquest shakes my hand. "Randall. And this is my son, Chet."

Chet. Jesus. These country club people don't even realize how ridiculous they are.

"Hey, Chet," I say. "You play a lot of tennis?"

Chet, with his perfectly coifed blond locks and his killer white smile, nods. "I played for Princeton."

I look at my mother. "And you told them that I haven't played in quite a while, right?"

"Of course, dear. But you're an athlete and you have my genes. You'll pick it right back up."

On what planet am I an athlete? Yes, my mother is a great player and is athletic, but I took after my dad. Maybe I should show them my rock climbing video, just to set the proper expectation.

Randall tosses my mother two balls, and they deftly disappear up her skirt. "Ladies first, Rosie," he says.

Ugh. My mother hates being called Rosie. It's Rosalyn. Rosalyn.

"Such a gentleman," she gushes, touching his chest. Ugh.

Chet and I make our way to our side of the court.

"I'll take backhand," he says. The strongest player always does, so I have no objection. But he could have asked me.

"No warm-up for me, huh?" I say.

My mother positions herself at the baseline and bounces the ball. "I'll take a few practice serves," she calls. "You can warm up that way."

Super.

She tosses the ball in the air and slams it my way. It hits the service box and goes by me before I can move.

"Good one!" I yell.

She serves and aces me again. I sigh.

"Are you ready?" Chet says. "Get on the balls of your feet. She's not serving that hard."

I give Chet my signature glare.

My mother hits another serve, and I lunge for it. The ball pings off the frame of my racquet and sails over the fence.

Chet sighs. My mother looks away.

"Okay," she calls. "This one's gonna count."

Great.

❧

Randall's like a big fat gorilla of a wall at the net. He actually stands in the middle, diving for every ball he can reach and slamming it at me.

This is not proper etiquette. When you play mixed doubles, yes, the men tend to make up for the women's weaknesses, but they are also supposed to hit to each other. When the helpless, weak woman on the other side is standing at the net, you do not hit an overhead at her. Period.

But no one told Randall that.

My mother slices a rather weak second serve to Chet, and since he's caught moving in the wrong direction, he barely manages to get the tip of his racquet on it and loop it over to his dad. I sigh and run backwards, knowing the ball is coming back at me.

Of course, I don't move fast enough. The ball hits the court about two feet in front of me and shoots up straight between my eyes, knocking my sunglasses off and my visor askew. I give them my back and try not to cry.

"You okay?" Chet says, actually putting a hand on my shoulder.

"Give me a sec," I manage.

"Shake it off," Randall calls across the court.

Shake it off? What kind of cretin is this guy?

It's my serve. Chet hands me my glasses, and I straighten my visor.

"Your face," he says. "Do you need some ice?"

"Thanks for the concern, Chet, but I'm shaking it off." He shakes his head and goes to his position at the net.

I get my first serve in and run to the net. My mother throws up a loopy ball, and I slam it with my forehand.

She claps her hand with her racquet. I actually hit a winner.

Now I'm serving to the gorilla.

I focus. I gather all my strength. I'm gonna hit it as hard as I can and hope for the best.

I actually hit a damn good serve, and Randall dumps it in the net. "Let!" he calls.

I look at Chet. *Let?* I mouth. There's no way that serve touched the net. Chet shrugs.

Fine.

I bounce the ball. I gather my strength again. And I fucking blast the serve.

And with a loud crack, it thuds right into Chet's back and he stumbles to the ground.

"Ow!" he cries. I run to him and kneel beside him.

"I'm so sorry," I say. "Are you okay?"

He shakes his head, and I watch a tear drip onto the court. "I'm not okay! It hurts!"

"Let me look at it." I lift his shirt, and sweet Jesus—he already has a purpling welt. "I think we need some ice."

Randall bounds over the net and to his son. "Chet? Tell Daddy where it hurts."

I pop to my feet and look at my mother, who has wandered up to the net. *Daddy?* I mouth. She shrugs.

Chapter 15

I'm running late. It's already ten 'til five when I race into the house and start the water for my shower. I throw my glasses and visor on the bed, strip off my sweat-soaked clothes, and head into the bathroom. But as I'm sliding open the shower door, I catch a glimpse of myself in the mirror.

Holy crap.

I lean over the counter, close to the mirror. I have an imprint of the edge of my glasses in my forehead and right between my eyes, and both my eyes are purple. I can't go in public like this!

I find my phone and call Martika. I can hear music in the background.

"Hey, where are you?" she says.

"I can't come," I say. "I got hit with a tennis ball in the face. I'm purple."

"Are you in pain?" she asks. "Do you need to go to the emergency room?"

"No," I say. "I'm fine, but it looks like I've been on the losing end of a bar brawl."

"But you're not in pain?"

"Well, the bruise is sore, but no."

"Then come," she says. "It'll be fun."

"Martika."

"Come on, Hope! Play the cool rock star. Put on some concealer, wear your shades with the mirrored lenses, and show some cleavage. No one will be looking at your face."

"Martika."

"Please," she says. "I think I'm liquored up enough to sing a Barry Manilow song. Pleeeease?"

"I'm not playing Barry Manilow," I say.

"Yes! Hurry up!"

ℬ

The party's in full swing. I can hear the laughter and music as soon as I get out of my car.

Benny's ten-year high school reunion is tomorrow night, and he invited a bunch of the out-of-towners here tonight. Martika's just about peed her pants in excitement. She can't wait to hear stories about nerdy Benny in high school.

I let myself in and almost bump into a wall, even though this place is like my second home. These damn sunglasses are too good. I grab a beer from the fridge and head out to the patio.

Martika squeals when she sees me. She gives me a big hug, bumping the guitar I have slung across my back.

"Thank you," she whispers in my ear. "I needed backup."

Ah. I should have known. Even in your own home, it's awkward to host ten people you don't know at all, but who know your husband.

"Can you see the bruise?" I whisper to her.

"Nope. You look divine. And much cooler than most of the people here."

"Are they not being nice?" I ask.

"No, they are," she says. "I shouldn't have said that. But you'll see what I mean."

Benny comes up and gives me a kiss on the cheek. He reeks of beer, and he's not a big drinker. But reunions tend to be tough to get through without alcohol.

He takes my arm and steers me to the center of the crowd.

"Everyone, this is our good friend, Hope!" he yells. The chatter stops, and everyone turns in our direction. "Turn off the music, Marti! Hope's gonna play!"

"Uh, everyone seems to be having fun, Ben," I say. "I can play later."

One of the men in the crowd approaches. He's tall, dark skinned, with wire-rimmed glasses and an untucked Oxford shirt. He's holding a glass of white wine, and he points it at me.

"Let's hear what you've got."

"Do you play?" I ask him.

He smiles. "I dabble."

I unsling my guitar and hold it out to him. "You first."

Benny claps and someone whistles and several others cheer. "Charles!" somebody cries.

"Come on, Charles," I say. "Light it up."

Charles holds up his hands to quiet the crowd. "I know one song. And I'm gonna give it to you." He looks at me. "Do you sing?"

"When the mood strikes."

He grins. "Let's see if we can get you in the mood."

Charles settles himself in a chair, and everyone gathers around. Chair legs scrape on the concrete, and Ben drags a bench closer. I sit on the concrete next to Martika, and Charles nods at me.

"It's Hope, right?"

"Yep."

"Let's see if I can give Hope something to sing about."

He thumps the guitar with the flat of his hand in a steady rhythm. Everyone claps along with him.

Where is he going with this?

And then he plays, strumming one string at a time, "Seven Nation Army" by The White Stripes.

I smile. It's the first "real" song a beginner learns because it's so easy and repetitive. Not to take away from Charles. The guy's got rhythm, and he knows how to work a crowd.

So I sing.

Martika pulls me to my feet, and we dance. Or thump. That's about all you can do with this song, but it's satisfying anyway. Benny joins us, thrashing his head and making a fool of himself. An endearing fool.

Charles laughs as he finishes the song, and he waves at me to take a bow.

"Nice," I say to him. "Very nice. You rocked it."

He stands and hands me the guitar. "Now I'm dying to hear you play. Let's hear your version of the same song."

"No way. I can't improve on it. I'll play something else."

Charles just shakes his head. "You're being polite."

"No, you were great. What else should I play?"

He raises an eyebrow. "You take requests?"

Benny throws an arm around my shoulders. "She does. Anything. Name any song. She'll kill it!"

God, I love Benny.

"How about KT Tunstall? 'Black Horse and the Cherry Tree'?" Charles says.

"I love that song!" Benny says.

"You gonna be my drums and my backup vocals?" I ask him.

Ben pumps a liquored fist in the air. "Yes!"

ೞ

I'm hot and sweaty, and I can feel the concealer caking on my face. Charles hands me a fresh beer, and I take it from him gratefully.

"So when does your album come out?" he asks.

We take a seat on the bench and sip. "Thank you for the compliment."

"I'm serious," he says. "I'd pay good money to listen to you."

I shake my head. "It's only a hobby."

"Jesus. What do you do for a living?"

I swallow my beer. "Technical writing. You?"

"Propulsion engineer. Way less exciting than it sounds."

I shift one leg under me on the bench. "Rockets or jets?"

"Rockets," he says. "Not many people know to ask that."

"Don't ask me anything else about it," I say. "That's all I know."

Charles smiles. "How long have you known Benny?"

"Five years," I say. "Since he and Martika started dating. I met her in the sixth grade. You?"

"Kindergarten," he says. "We both grew up in the same shitty neighborhood, but both of us pulled ourselves out. I admire the hell out of the guy."

"Me, too," I say. "He's great for Marti. She's very lucky."

Charles slugs his beer. "Are you married?"

I shake my head. "You?"

He smiles. "Not a lot of women in my field. I thought I'd have plenty of time after college to start my career and find someone, but it hasn't happened."

"Life rarely goes where we expect it."

He gives me a searching look. "Sounds like there's a story there."

I shrug. "I'm currently in the process of finding myself. I only recently realized I'm missing."

Charles laughs. He's got a great laugh. "You're an incredible musician. Why aren't you doing something with it?" I stay silent. "Or is that a personal question?"

"It is, but…my dad is Joe Cruz. The music's in my soul, but I'll be damned if I walk his path."

Charles stares at me. And then he slowly nods. "I can understand that."

"What about you? When did you start playing guitar?"

"Last week," he says. "I always wanted to learn, but we didn't have the money when I was young, and then I got too busy...I'm making time. Time for the important things."

"I can understand that."

We smile at each other. And then Charles shakes his head.

"What?" I ask.

"I feel like the universe is playing with me. I finally meet a hot woman with brains who I'm interested in, and she lives halfway across the country."

My cheeks grow warm. "Thanks."

"If I even knew I could be out here every month, I'd ask you out. Hell, I'd skip the reunion for a date with you."

I lean forward and kiss his cheek. "I'd say yes."

Then he puts a hand up to my cheek. "Can I take the glasses off?"

"Uh. Actually...it's kinda funny. I was playing tennis today and I got hit right between the eyes. It's not pretty."

"I bet I don't even notice," he says.

I debate...and then I nod.

He slides my glasses off and we stare into each other's eyes. And then Charles kisses me softly.

Mmm. He's warm and soft and perfect.

"If you ever get back out to California, look me up," I say.

Benny stumbles over to us, interrupting. He slings an arm over each of our shoulders from behind the bench and leans in close. "Marti has told me it's time for bed. She's already there. It's midnight, and she has to work in the morning."

Charles and I exchange a smile. "Walk me out?" I say.

I kiss Benny goodnight, and out we go.

Chapter 16

"I'm not tired at all," Charles says as he walks me to my car. "It's two in Houston. I should be out."

"Me either," I say. I turn to him. "Thanks for the talk. And the songs. I had a great time."

"Me, too," he says. "I meant what I said."

"Well." I take a deep breath. "We could continue. Talking, I mean. At my place."

He blinks. "You're sure? I don't know when I can visit. If I can ever visit."

"I understand."

He smiles. "I have my rental car. I'll follow you."

৪১

I make us each a cup of coffee, and we settle on my couch.

"Big place for one person," he says.

I nod. "Hoping to fill it with a family someday."

"How many kids do you want?"

"Ten."

Charles's eyes go wide, and he laughs. "Shit, that's a baseball team."

I laugh with him. "I was an only child. It was lonely. I want a big, loud, messy family. What about you?"

"I'm the baby of seven," he says, "so I'm leaning towards two. A nice, neat, round, manageable number."

"Seven," I say. "What was that like?"

"Chaos. I had three extra mothers with my overbearing sisters, and my brothers just wreaked havoc. Two were dead before they could graduate high school."

"I'm so sorry."

He shakes his head. "It's not what you think. Sickle cell anemia. Runs in my family. Even though we were poor, my parents stayed together, and they ruled with an iron fist. If I stepped a toe out of line, I was punished. But it worked. All five us went to college. We're all successful. I hope I can give my kids the same thing."

"They sound like amazing people," I say. "I love to hear stories of happy families."

I sip my coffee, and Charles cocks his head. "Was yours not happy?"

"No. My dad was a drug addict. He beat me and my mom. But hey, I got a steady stream of guitar and piano lessons out of the deal."

Charles sets his coffee down and takes my free hand in his. "You have beautiful hands."

I smile at him. He puts his lips to my knuckles and kisses them softly. My stomach flip-flops.

I set my own coffee down and shift closer to him. Our knees bump. Our eyes meet. My stomach rolls again, like I'm flying in a roller coaster, and I lean in and place my lips on his.

Charles is slow, lazy, almost, in the way he kisses. He takes his time, deepening the kiss and pulling me closer before he opens his mouth and gives me his sweet, soft tongue.

Oh. I melt into him. He holds my face in his hands and works that tongue slowly, so slowly, exploring every part of my mouth. I run my hands up his neck and into his hair, and he sighs into my mouth.

It's the slowest I've ever made love, and it's delicious. Charles takes his time, exploring my neck, my breasts, my stomach, my thighs, until we're finally on the bed, and he's over me, moving his hips in a slow, sensual rhythm that thrills every part of me.

Our mouths never part. In one smooth motion, he's deep inside of me, and we move together, two people who've connected on every level, who are connected, and he makes love to me for hours, literally hours, until we fall asleep welded together.

I wake alone, late for work, but I don't care. There's a note on my pillow.

You're walking your own path, Hope, and I'm so lucky to have stumbled across it. Call me. Any time. I'll dream about this night forever. Yours, Charles

I hold the note to my heart and force myself out of bed.

Chapter 17

"So update me on the last month," Dr. Steinburg says.

"I went rock climbing," I say. "It was okay, but not for me."

"In the interest of honesty," he says, "I have to tell you...your mother sent me a link to the video."

I sigh, and he laughs.

"At least you tried."

I nod. "I did. And I met someone else."

"Wow," he says. "I can't believe it. I mean, I can, but—"

I laugh. "I get it. I can't believe it, either."

"Do you want to share?"

"He's a friend of a friend and...I'll just admit it. I slept with him the night we met."

"And?"

"And he lives in Houston. His job doesn't allow much travel. We've been emailing, though."

"Is that what you want? A long-distance relationship?"

"Not really, but we don't have a lot of choice."

"Except that your job allows for travel, at least on weekends. And you have the money to go."

I nod. "I know."

"So something is holding you back."

"It's not him," I say. "He's…close to perfect. Smart and funny and sweet and easy to talk to. But my life is here. I don't want to move."

"Is that a deal breaker? Moving?"

I shrug. "I don't know. I want to say no, but the thought of leaving…it makes me sick."

"Why?"

"I don't know."

"If you say 'I don't know' one more time, I will throw you out," Dr. Steinburg says, his voice firm. "You are an adult, and you have a sound mind. Use it."

"But I honestly don't know," I say. "How do I figure out if moving is what I want?"

"You weigh the pros and cons," he says. "Do you want to be with this man?"

I nod. "I could be. If he were here, we'd definitely be dating."

"Can you live with only seeing him once or twice a month?"

I close my eyes and lean my head back. What do I really want? What can I live with?

"I think I met him too early," I finally say. "I haven't got my life figured out yet, and there are too many big decisions that would need to be made with him. I'm not ready for him."

Dr. Steinburg smiles. "That's a good answer."

"It is?"

We both laugh.

"You're making progress," he says. "And you're getting stronger. But you're not there yet. I think you should take any relationship slowly. Now, what about the guitar? Are you playing every day?"

I nod. "New stuff. Not the old, but I'm hopeful I'll get there."

"And why can't you play the old?"

"It just reminds me too much of Matt."

"Let's talk about that. What was right about your marriage?"

"We knew each other," I say. "I mean, all the little stuff, the quirks and the insecurities and the pet peeves and the likes and dislikes."

I get the stare and a nod.

"And...we were both supportive of each other. Of what we wanted to do in our lives. And I was comfortable with him."

"So to recap, you said WE knew each other, and WE were supportive, and that YOU were comfortable. What about Matt? Was he comfortable? And don't even think about telling me you don't know."

I shrug. "I thought so. But since you put it in my head that maybe he left because he couldn't be himself...no. I don't think he was comfortable. He walked on egg shells around me, didn't he?"

"You tell me."

I nod. "He did."

"Let me ask you something. Why did you never get help for your issues?"

"I couldn't face it," I say. "I was embarrassed, ashamed, angry, hurt. I just tried to ignore the whole thing."

"Did Matt ever encourage you to get help?"

"He tried. He even paid a psychologist to come to our house once. I just refused to talk."

"So what made this time different?"

I take a deep breath. "I needed a way to get my music back."

Dr. Steinburg refills his coffee mug from the pot on the table between us. "Did you and Matt have a conversation at the end? Did he explain why he left?"

"It wasn't much of a conversation," I say. "He said he loved me, completely, but that he needed to move on. He said we'd gotten married too young. I found out two weeks later that he'd been seeing someone."

"Do you think he was being honest?"

"You think he didn't really love me?" I ask.

"No, I don't think that. But I think there's more to the story. From what you've told me, Matt hated to hurt you. Perhaps there were other reasons he needed to go, but he was afraid to tell you. Do you think this is a possibility?"

Tears gather in my eyes. I nod.

"Do you think you're strong enough to hear the truth? If Matt were willing to give it to you?"

"I don't know" is on the tip of my tongue. But that's a lie. I do know.

"Yes."

"Then that's it. You need to ask him. If you don't know what went wrong, how can you fix it?"

Chapter 18

I gather my courage and call Matt at work. I figure he won't be able to tell it's me calling, and maybe I have a shot at speaking to him.

It goes to voicemail. I leave a bland, not-desperate message, asking him to call me back.

Martika calls just as I put my phone down.

"Hey. How's therapy?"

I smile. "Good. Going good."

"Benny just got off the phone with Charles. He says he's gonna try to come out next month."

I sit down and put my head between my knees. "That's good."

"What's wrong?" she asks. "I thought you liked him."

"I like him a lot," I say, lifting my head. "I think I just moved too fast."

"A rendezvous once a month is not what I'd call fast."

"No, but he's a keeper. And I'm not ready to keep anyone."

Martika doesn't say anything. I can hear her washing dishes.

"You're right," she finally says. "You just need to have fun. No commitments, no strings."

"Does that sound like me?"

She laughs. "I thought we didn't know you. You could be anyone. Maybe you're Batgirl."

I smile. "I'd rather be Wonder Woman."

"That's it!" she cries. "Thank you!"

"That's what? Thank you for what?"

"I need a birthday present for Ben next week. I'll buy him rope."

"Rope?" I say with a laugh. "Why the hell would you buy him rope?"

"So I can tie him up. It'll be a blast."

I shake my head. "Benny's a lucky man."

"Isn't he, though?"

I laugh again. "My mom's probably having a hissy. I was supposed to meet her ten minutes ago."

"For what? I thought you always see her on Sundays."

"Dinner with Randall," I say in best British accent. "He wishes to dine as a family."

"Is Randall *Daddy*?"

I giggle. "Yep."

"This should be fun. Is his wussy son joining you?"

"But of course. He must be present to pull out my chair and so that I have something to dab at with my napkin."

Martika cackles. "Let me know how it goes. And wear the heels. Why did you buy them if you never wear them?"

"I'm going. Thanks, *Mom*."

"Bye."

&

Dinner at the club, promptly at eight. So of course my mother makes me arrive at seven.

We order drinks and sit at the bar while we wait.

"So what's up with Randall?" I ask. "It's not getting serious, is it?"

"What shoes are you wearing? You're like a giant."

I hold out one leg and we both look down. "Hooker heels. Marti made me buy them."

Mom wrinkles her nose. "Really, Hope, do you have to use that language?"

"What fucking language is that?"

"Shhh!" she whispers furiously. "We're not at a saloon! Lower your voice."

I lean into her. "Why are you acting like this, like you actually like this place? Dinner at the country club? That's not who you are."

"I'm having fun with a nice man," she says, straightening her lapel. "Nothing wrong with that."

"You don't need his money."

"But why should I spend mine if I can spend his?"

I stare at her. And then we both laugh.

She waves a hand. "I'm not serious. He's not even that rich. But he treats me well. So he's an ass on the tennis court. Everyone has flaws."

"Some more than others," I say, and she swats my arm.

"Be nice. Chet is quite accomplished. You might have something in common."

"Doubtful."

"He's been coddled all his life, and he is a product of his childhood. You should recognize each other."

"No one ever coddled me."

My mother sighs. "Why are you being so difficult? They're both nice. Give it a chance."

"So you want me to chalk up their poor behavior to Randall's competitive nature and Chet's childhood?"

"You nailed him," she says, lowering her voice. "Randall sent me pictures of the bruise. It was awful."

I try to keep the smile off my face. "Do you still have them?"

She looks stealthily about the room, ensuring we're alone. Then she takes out her phone and starts scrolling.

"Here."

I rear my head back. "Holy Christ. I did that?"

"I told you you were athletic."

"Poor guy. No one deserves that."

The bartender takes my empty iced tea glass and gives me another. "No one deserves what?"

My mother holds up her phone. "Look what my daughter did. On a serve. Hit her partner square in the back. He cried."

The bartender winces. "Anyone I know?"

Mom opens her mouth, but then closes it and puts her phone away. "No. Pity. Hurt so bad he may never play again."

The bartender grins at me and goes back to his work.

"He may never play again?" I say. "Where do you get this shit?"

She smiles. "It's fun. You're right, I don't really belong here, so I can be anyone I want. It's like acting. I always wanted to be an actress."

"Since when?"

"Since always," she says. "You don't know every little thought I've ever had."

"Thank God."

"Oh. There they are. Sit up straight. They're coming."

I hike my skirt a little higher and twist my stool sideways. It never hurts to show a little leg.

ഗ

Randall kisses my mother's cheek and then kisses mine. "You both look beautiful," he says. "I'm sorry about your..." He waves a hand at me. "I get a little carried away when I play a game. Call me the stereotypical male."

"Guess I should bow out of the after-dinner Monopoly, then," I say, and he laughs.

"I'm truly sorry. Thank you for having a sense of humor about it."

Chet steps up. I give him my hand, which he squeezes, and then he leans in for a cheek kiss anyway. He smells expensive.

"How's the back?" I ask him.

"Sore," he says. "But at least I can hide it."

"I picked this dress because it's the same shade as my bruise," I say. "At least I match."

"Our table's ready whenever we are," Randall says. "Shall we?"

Mom slides off her stool and takes his proffered arm. Chet offers me his, and we head back to the dining room.

Chet pulls out my chair for me. I smile at him, and he slides it in smoothly under my butt.

We take our menus from the waiter. "What do you recommend, Chet?"

"The salmon is excellent," he says. "The scallops, too. Do you like seafood?"

"Sometimes," I say.

"What are you in the mood for?"

He suggested salmon and scallops. So I'm debating between them, but they aren't actually what I want.

"Beef, I think."

Randall chuckles. "Where will you put it, in that dress? Try the house salad with shrimp."

I glance at my mother. I get nothing.

"I think I'll have beef, too," Chet says, looking hard at his menu. "The short ribs melt in your mouth."

"I need potatoes with that," I say. "Should I go mashed or au gratin?"

"You pick one and I'll order the other," he says. "We can share."

I smile at him and close my menu. "What do you do for a living?"

"Real estate attorney," he says.

"Chet just made partner last year," Randall says. "The youngest at the firm."

Our waiter steps up and asks for our drink order.

"Margarita," I say. "Blended." My mother and Randall look at me in horror.

"Make that two," Chet says.

Randall orders a bottle of Chateau St. Something for them to split, and as soon as the waiter leaves, he leans across the table.

"I'm sorry, but you'll have to do without the free chips and salsa."

"How do you know about those?" I ask. "You mean, you've been to that type of place before? Mother, did you know this?"

Chet fights to hide his laughter behind his napkin.

My mother narrows her eyes. "Please stop. This is supposed to be a nice family dinner. We don't have to push each other's buttons now, do we?"

"What's your business, Randy?" I ask.

The muscles in his jaw clench. "I specialize in second-hand parts for automobiles."

I can't think of single comeback for that. "Sounds interesting."

"He's been in television commercials," my mother says.

"Oh. Really? Which ones?"

"For my business," Randall says. "Just some local spots."

"Would I have seen them?"

Chet smiles. And then he sings. "Grab and go, so you don't get snowed, it's the Grab and Go Junkyaaaard!"

I laugh. "No way! You're the Junk Man!"

"Laugh all you want, but it's a very lucrative business."

"I'm not laughing at you," I say. "You have to admit, those commercials are funny."

Randall cracks a smile. "If you remembered the jingle, they did the trick."

The waiter returns with our drinks and takes our order. While my mother and Randall talk, I'm left with Chet.

Which has turned out to be far more entertaining than I anticipated.

"So what do you do?" he asks.

"Nothing important," I say. "I'm thinking about a career change."

"What would you like to do?"

"Music," I admit.

"Tough one," he says. "I can see you've been raised with money and class, but it's exhausting, isn't it? I wish I had the kind of creative talent that would allow a career like that."

"You do?"

He laughs. "Why the surprise?"

"You just seem to fit in here very well."

"If you hadn't ordered the margarita, I would have thought you fit here, too."

I look around. "Yeah, I grew up with money. I can fit in here, but like you said, it's exhausting."

"What do you want to do with music? Do you sing?"

"Some. I write songs and play the guitar, the bass, keys...mostly guitar. But I don't know if I want to do my own stuff or write for someone else."

"Thirteen years of piano lessons here," he says. "In some ways I'm grateful, but I never connected to it."

"You learned the classical stuff?"

"Exclusively," he says.

"What kind of music do you like?"

He leans into my ear. "Country."

I smile. "Maybe you should learn some country songs."

"Only if I wanted to give my father a heart attack."

"How good are you?" I ask.

Chet smiles. "I can play Beethoven's 'Hammerklavier' pretty well."

I laugh. "That's some major shit, right there."

"Have you ever played it?"

I grab his hand and pull him up. "Let's try something."

"Where are you two going?" my mother asks.

We push our chairs in. "We'll be right back," I tell her.

I lead Chet over to the piano in the corner of the room. I slide onto the bench and pat the seat next to me.

He shakes his head. "We can't do this. They'll kick us out."

"Not if we're good," I say.

He reluctantly sits. "You are outrageous."

"If they make us leave, I'll buy you a beer and hot wings."

Chet laughs. "You're on."

"Okay. What's your favorite country song?"

"'The Dance' by Garth Brooks."

"That's perfect for piano," I say. "Give me a sec to get the tune in my head."

I close my eyes and put my fingers on the keys. I play without playing, moving my hands to make sure I've got the song right.

I open my eyes. "Okay. It starts here. E-B-E-F#—"

"Wait," he says. "How do you know that?"

"I hear it. I hear a note and I know what it is."

"Wow. Okay. I can't do that, but I can follow along."

"We'll do it in eight-note increments," I say. "I'll play it, you play it, then we'll play it together."

And as I play the first eight notes, my mother marches over to us. "What are you doing?"

"Teaching him his favorite song," I say.

"You can't do that! Not in the middle of dinner!"

Everyone in the dining room is looking at us. So I stand up.

"Excuse me. I hate to interrupt your meals, but I'm going to spend about ten minutes teaching this man to play a beautiful song. And then I will play the song in its entirety. I think we need a little music."

Then a man in a tuxedo comes over. "I'm the manager here. What's going on?"

Chet stands. "Why is there no music evening? I come here quite frequently, and someone usually plays while we dine."

"Our pianist cancelled. I apologize, sir, but I can't have you—"

Chet pulls the man to the side. I watch him slip the guy a Ben Franklin.

"Perhaps to set the mood," the manager says, "you could play something to soothe the crowd."

Chet looks at me.

"I know the perfect thing," I say.

So I play a little Barry Manilow.

❧

Chet gives me a hug at my car. "Thanks for an audacious evening."

I hug him back, sincerely, and he winces. "Sorry!" I say. "Did I hurt you again?"

He nods and laughs. "Are you seeing anyone?"

Uh oh. "Not really."

"Are you up for a blind date?"

I raise an eyebrow. "A blind date?"

"My…the person I'm seeing, they have a friend. I think you'd be perfect together. We can do beer and wings."

"Will you promise to wear jeans?"

He hesitates. "I promise nothing."

I laugh and kiss his cheek. "Call me. I'd love to hang out."

❧

My mother calls me as soon as I pull into traffic.

"I don't know whether to laugh or cry right now," she says.

"Laugh. Crying will ruin your makeup."

"Oh you! Randall was so embarrassed! I don't think he'll ever come here again!"

"His loss," I say. "The food is great."

"Will you just stop?" she yells. "He broke up with me!"

I cringe. Even if I think Randall is an asshole, I didn't mean to hurt my mother. "I'm sorry, Ma."

"If you think he'll let you and Chet be together, think again."

"Me and Chet?" I say. "Chet's gay."

"He...what?"

"Didn't you see him singing along to *Mandy*?"

"That's a stereotype," she says. "Not all gay men love Barry Manilow."

"But how many straight men do?"

She sighs. "Poor Chet. No wonder Randall's up his ass."

"Randall doesn't know," I say. "And don't you dare say anything. Chet needs to handle it."

"Why would he tell you something like that? You've known each other for two minutes."

"He didn't tell me," I say. "He just...he stumbled over a couple of things, and I just know. I'll find out for sure next weekend. He's gonna set me up with one of his friends."

"That sounds promising."

I shrug. "Anyway, I'm sorry Randall's gone, but I think you're better off."

"Yeah, I guess. Back to the drawing board."

Chapter 19

It's past eleven when I get home. I wash my face, gently, brush my teeth, and throw on some sweats. My phone rings just as I sink under the covers.

Matt.

My heart starts thumping.

"Hey," I say.

"Hi," he says. "I just got your message. Is it too late?"

"No, I just got home. Thanks for returning my call. How's the head?"

"Fine. What's up?"

"Um…I have a couple questions for you, but I'd like to talk in person."

"I don't think that's a good idea," he says. "Can we just talk now?"

"Okay." I shift higher against my pillows. "First…I want to thank you."

He hesitates. "For what?"

"For being so good to me. I'd be dead without you, Matt. Literally. You saved me, and you gave me love when not even my parents did, and I've just never thanked you for that."

Matt stays quiet.

"And the reason I'm saying this is that I never realized what that might have cost you. I never thought about it, but since I've been going to therapy…I'm seeing everything differently."

"You're going to therapy?"

"Yeah. Too little, too late, I know. But I'm learning, and I'm really looking at myself, and I need to know."

"Know what?"

"Exactly why you left."

Matt sighs. "It's done, Hope. We don't need to go there. I appreciate the thanks, and I'm glad you're getting help, but it's over."

"I know," I say. "I know it's over. But I'm asking for this one last favor. I don't want to make the same mistakes. Please. Just give me honesty."

"Don't do this," he says. "I don't want to hurt you. Let's move on."

"I can't!" I scream. "I can't move on until I know what went wrong. Please tell me. I can handle it."

"You already know. I know you know."

"I can guess," I say. "Is that what you need me to do?"

"Go for it."

I sit up and push the hair from my eyes. "You couldn't be yourself with me. I was so fragile that you had to tiptoe around me, and a lot of your energy just went into making sure I was emotionally stable. And you were willing to work with me, but you wanted me to help myself, and I just refused. You wanted me to have my own thoughts and opinions, and to make a choice every once in a while, but I couldn't. All the decisions, from the mortgage down to where we ate dinner, you had to make every single one. You were exhausted." I pause. "Stop me when I say something that doesn't ring a bell."

"You're doing pretty good," he says.

"And there were other things, little things, like maybe we weren't that passionate about sex anymore, and we were way too comfortable and things were too routine…but it comes down to me. I was a mess."

Matt blows out a loud breath. "You weren't a mess."

"I was," I say. "I still am. But I'm facing it. Finally."

We sit in silence. I'm using Dr. Steinburg's trick—when you want someone to talk, you shut up.

"Part of it was me," he says. "I knew all those things about you, and I accepted them a long time ago. But it got harder and harder to deal with them. I wasn't strong enough for you."

"Don't say that," I say. "Don't make excuses for me. You did way more than you had to, and I did nothing. I gave very little. And I'm so sorry for that."

"You gave," he says. "You loved me, and I always knew it, always felt it. I never doubted you once. I don't think many men can say that about their wives."

"Thanks. That's all. I didn't mean to bring up old shit. I just wanted to make sure I'm on the right track, and that you know…I know how good you are. I know I fucked up something really good."

"Hope…I'm glad you're getting help. I'm glad that things are getting better."

"Me, too," I say. "Sweet dreams."

"Sweet dreams."

Chapter 20

So I'm sitting here after work, in my dry-clean-only clothes, watching a demonstration of how to throw a pot. I mean, come on. Everyone's seen *Ghost*. It looks easy, right?

The wheels we have are electric, almost like a sewing machine—step on the pedal, and the wheel turns.

"Start off slow," the instructor says. "You have to be in control. But this is physics. If the wheel turns too slowly, the clay will fall."

Why is every activity I try about physics?

I get my hands nice and wet and moisten the mound of clay in front of me. Ooooh, it feels kinda cool. I like this. I rub my hands over and over the clay, just enjoying the sensation.

"All your effort is being wasted on a chunk of clay that can't feel anything," the instructor says.

I slit open one eye (I hadn't realized I'd closed them), and look down. Wow. I've fondled the hell out of the clay.

"Sorry," I say. "I've never done this before."

"You don't say?"

She moves on and I scowl at her behind her back.

Fine. No more playing around. A masterpiece is waiting to be created.

I mold the clay into a vague bowl-like shape, without the actual bowl part. Then I give a tentative tap on the pedal. The wheel spins half-heartedly and the clay doesn't move.

Right. I need to mold it as I go. I need to be bold, give the pedal a little juice.

I press down again, keeping my hands tight around the clay. The clay starts to climb above my hands, getting taller and thinner. Cool.

Except I want a bowl.

I take my foot off the pedal and the clay collapses in on itself. I wet it some more, remold it into my mound shape, and start the wheel again. This time, I keep my fingers around the top and press down, trying to get a concave depression.

"That's good," my instructor says over my shoulder, and I jump. "You'll need to go faster to get the bowl shape."

"Like this?"

"A bit more. Keep your hands around the rim. A bit more."

I give it a bit more, and my nose itches. Without thinking, I rub it, smearing watery clay over half my face, and, I don't know, there must be a real ghost in here or something, because my foot presses down all the way on the pedal and the clay whips out with a moist squelch and plasters the face of the girl sitting next to me.

My dirty hands automatically cover my mouth.

"Oh, Christ," my instructor says.

Chapter 21

"It's just the gym," Martika says for the twelfth time. "You have to exercise."

"I refuse to leave the house," I say. "The gym's a dangerous place. I could kill somebody."

"Oh come on," she says. "Stop being so dramatic. You've had a few accidents, that's all."

"I don't need an accident at the gym," I say. "I could drop a weight on your foot and crush your toe. Or maybe my socks will get tangled in the gears of the stationary bike and I'll have a mangled ankle. Or I could slip on a sweaty mat and break my leg. I'm not going."

"This new you is not an improvement."

I roll my eyes, even though she can't see me. "You only say that 'cause you can't bully me anymore."

Martika gasps. "Do you mean that?"

"Shit, Marti, I'm sorry," I say. "Of course I don't mean that. Bad joke."

"Yeah. Okay. I'll talk to you later."

"Marti—"

But she's already hung up.

I flop back on the couch. Actually...it was only sort of a joke. There's some truth to it.

I wouldn't call Martika a bully, but she's used to coaxing me into things, whether I want to do them or not. I always give in. And that's on me, but she's having a tough time with it. I'm not the Go-Along Girl anymore.

I thought that maybe I had to face my loss of Matt to find my music again. I prepared myself for that, for turning sadness and grief into self-righteous anger so that I could move on.

I did not expect to look deep within and find a serious need to change.

And even now...you'd think an internal change would be just that: internal. But it's affecting everything and everyone around me.

Figures.

Chapter 22

"You're becoming quite the YouTube sensation," Dr. Steinburg says.

I wrinkle my brow. "Huh?"

"You…didn't you know?"

"You mean the rock climbing video? Yeah, I knew that."

"That's all you've seen?" he asks.

My eyes widen. "You mean, there's more?"

He takes his tablet off the table. "This is from one of those gossip sites. Quote, 'Joe Cruz's daughter is coming out of the shadows. Dinner at the club turns into a mini concert for these lucky diners. We're not surprised she's so good with those Cruz genes, but we are surprised that no one knew about it.' End quote."

"I…how did they know it was me?"

"They're reporters," he says. "They dig. And then apparently you took a pottery class?"

"How did you know that?"

He taps on his tablet. "'Hope Cruz Nails Another One,' is the headline." He flips the screen towards me so I can see it.

"Someone videotaped that?" I shriek. "What the fuck? This is your fault. If you hadn't insisted that I find a hobby, I'd still be anonymous."

Dr. Steinburg gives me a scathing look. "Really?"

I sigh. "Fine. I take it back. But this is ridiculous."

"I'm surprised it didn't happen sooner," he says. "Have you never had to deal with it?"

I shrug. "Not really. Ever since my dad died...my mom laid low. I've never even attended a concert as an adult, at least not until a few months ago."

"I have celebrity clients, Hope," he says. "It's a complication, but it can be dealt with."

"How? On one hand, I'm trying not to hide anymore. I'm trying to admit who I am. But I don't want to be famous or followed."

"Then explain this mini concert in the restaurant," he says. "What was going through your head?"

"I didn't know someone would tape me."

Patient stare.

"I was rebelling. And the only real way I can do that is with my music. It's the only area of my life where I have complete confidence."

"Did you enjoy it?"

I nod. "Maybe too much."

"Then you'll have to decide. There are consequences to our actions. Performing will bring attention. Attention may be too much. You have to decide."

I scowl. Decisions suck.

Chapter 23

My phone rings while I'm eating lunch at my desk. When I pick it up, I see the call is from Matt's mother.

My hands start shaking. I haven't spoken to her in months, but I've missed her.

"Hello?" I say.

"Hi, Hope. It's Jan. Is this a good time?"

"Hi, Jan. Sure. What's up?"

"I've been meaning to call…I want to apologize. I should have kept in touch."

"I get it," I say. "You don't have to apologize. He's your son."

"But you've always been my daughter," she says, her voice breaking. "I shouldn't have abandoned you."

I put my forehead down on the desk. "I appreciate that."

"Someone sent me a link to a video. The one where you're playing the piano? And I took it as a sign. I just want you to know you're in my prayers."

I smile at that. "I learned Barry Manilow for you."

"I know," she says. "Anyway, I just want you to know I'm here. I know it might be weird, us having a relationship, and I wrestled with it, but…I don't care. I'm willing. So if you are…"

"Let's stay in touch," I say. "It is kinda weird, though. And I don't know how Matt will feel about it."

"He's the one that sent me the link," she says. "I guess I thought I was being loyal, but to whom? We've been a part of each other's lives for so long. I don't want to lose that."

Huh. Matt sent her the video?

"Maybe we can have lunch," I say. "I'll call you next week."

"Thank you, Hope. I miss you and I love you."

Tears sting my eyes. "I love you, too."

෨

What the hell was that?

Why would Matt send her that video? He divorced me. Why does he even care what I'm doing? I mean, he wouldn't even meet me face to face, and now he wants me to have a relationship with his mom?

Okay, I made that up. Jan didn't say that. But he started it.

I think about Jan and Matt's dad, Jim. They took care of me. I never really let Jan in, but she knew what I was going through at home anyway. She soothed my bruises, cleaned up some of the nastier cuts, even took me to her private doctor when my dad pushed me down the stairs and broke my arm. That was the day my mother finally moved us out.

And I suddenly realize that part of my sadness is from losing them. The only loving parental figures I've ever known.

And I wonder what that says about me. How completely out of touch with my own feelings am I?

Chapter 24

Chet offers to pick me up for our group date, and then he changes his mind.

"Actually, maybe you should drive yourself. In case you want to make a fast getaway."

"That really doesn't inspire confidence in the man you've chosen," I say, and he laughs.

"I'm thinking of you," he says. "But if you want me to drive…"

"You don't even know me and you know me," I say. "I'll drive myself. See you there."

"Ciao."

I look in the mirror for the tenth time and wipe the goo from the corners of my eyes. Looking good. Got my tight jeans on, a sexy off-the-shoulder sweater with hot pink bra just in case the strap shows, and my hooker heels.

Feeling good. I know Chet's got my back, I'm just living for the moment, and I'm ready to have fun.

And then a thought occurs to me.

This will be man number three in as many months. Seems like a high ratio, I mean, a guy a month? Isn't that a lot?

On the other hand, if I average it out, say, over the last twelve years, assuming I would have started dating at sixteen…that's only one guy every 36 months. That sounds a lot more reasonable.

Okay. I'm not a slut. I'm just a girl, meeting a guy. There's no guarantee I'll even like him, let alone sleep with him. In fact, that's a promise I'm making to myself right now: I won't sleep with him. No matter who is or what he looks like or how he makes me feel. I will resist!

Maybe.

∛

I walk in The Office from its strip-mall entrance expecting a little dive (not that I've been to many dives). But this place is plush—leather booths, Tiffany lamps, mahogany paneling, and a huge bar a la Cheers, complete with spit-shined brass rails. Cool.

Chet sees me and waves. All three men in the booth scoot out to stand like the gentlemen they are.

"Beautiful," Chet says as he gives me a hug. "You look beautiful."

"Thanks. You, too," I whisper back.

"This is my better half, Clancy," and I take his hand and shake it firmly, "and this is Spencer Giles. He works with Clancy at Mayberry & Foster."

I raise an eyebrow at Spencer as he shakes my hand. "Entertainment lawyer?"

"You know our firm?"

"I'm a client."

The three of them stare at me.

"I didn't know you did anything with your music, Hope," Chet says.

"It's not for my work," I say. "My mother and I hold the rights to a valuable catalog. I usually don't say anything, but I guess you'll find out anyway...Joe Cruz. Joe Cruz is my father."

"Holy shit," Chet says. "Did my father know that?"

I give him a small smile. "I'm guessing not."

Clancy laughs. "Let's sit and get a drink. I don't work on your account, but I wish I did, 'cause I could write this bar tab off."

Spencer looks down at me, even though I'm wearing those heels of death. He must be six foot four. "I don't work on your account, either, Hope. But if this is awkward for you, I understand."

"I'm fine with it," I say. "Sit."

He slides into the booth and I sit beside him.

"Ever dated a client?"

He shakes his head. "Ever dated a lawyer?"

"Nope. But I have a couple of questions. Maybe if I ask them you can write this tab off."

Spencer laughs. "No business. I just got off work and it's eight o'clock on a Saturday night. So music runs in the family, huh?"

I nod. "Does lawyering run in yours?"

"Fourth generation," he says. "My great-grandfather was a London barrister."

"So do you actually like your job or was it just a given?"

"Both. I took some heat for going into entertainment, but it's where my contacts took me. Clancy and I roomed at Yale. He had an uncle in film, an older cousin on Broadway, and it just made sense." He shrugs.

"So you represent actors?" I ask.

"No, actually. I ended up in the software division. Mostly video game companies and associated contracts."

He pushes up his glasses with a knuckle and clears his throat. He looks kind of...embarrassed.

"Do you play video games?" I ask.

"So," Clancy says, butting in. "Here's our server. What's your pleasure?"

They all order Stella. I stick to my guns and order a Corona.

I turn back to Spencer. "So...video games?"

Then Chet leans in. "I told them the story of our first meeting," he says. "Good Lord. Not a great day for my father."

I notice Clancy sit back and scowl.

"Well, I sympathize with you there," I say. "You and I, we needed to look elsewhere for positive male role models."

"That's the fucking understatement of the century," Clancy says, and Chet sighs.

"So video games," I say again, and Chet moves to speak. I lean over the table and zip his mouth shut with my finger. "Shut it. Let the man speak."

Spencer looks like he wants to barf. "Grown men rarely play video games," he says.

"In my experience, it's the opposite," I say. "I have a few *World of Warcraft* toons. I mean, who doesn't?"

Clancy laughs out loud.

Our beers arrive, and I scoop up mine and Spencer's before he can protest. I stand. "Can you guys give us a minute? Spencer and I need to have a chat."

∽

I lead Spencer over to another booth and plop down. He sits across from me and takes his beer.

"I'm gonna be sort of a bitch, and I hope you take it the right way, but if you don't, fair enough."

His eyes go wide. "Okay."

"I used to be just like you, hiding who I was and what I wanted and what I liked, thinking I needed to be someone else for everyone else. But let me tell you, and this is experience talking…it doesn't work. Now maybe you don't like the look of me, or the sound of me, or hell, the smell of me. Fine. We might never see each other again. But we came here with the expectation of getting to know each other. And we can't do that if we're not honest."

He picks at the label on his beer bottle.

"If you like video games, own it. If you want a glass of wine instead of beer, order it. Fifty years from now, do you want to be drinking Stella?"

Spencer cracks a smile. "Not really."

I laugh. "Chet means well, I know. He was trying very hard to keep you from telling me about the video games you play. But if I decided I didn't like you because you enjoy a certain activity…well, I wouldn't be the right girl for you."

"I play *World of Warcraft*, too," he says. "Name a video game system, and I have it. I can blow you away at *MarioKart*."

I smile. "I'll take that challenge."

He laughs hard. "I'm sorry, Hope. I don't date much."

"Why's that?"

"My job, and…I'm not good at this. Clancy and I go to a bar, and all the women flock to him. And he's not even interested."

I take a hard look at the package in front of me. Spencer looks put together, monied, decently handsome. Not a showstopper, but hey, neither am I, nor are most people, for that matter.

"I think you look great," I say. "And you're nice, you've kept the conversation going. You have a great job and you dress well. Maybe Clancy just likes all the attention."

Spencer laughs. "Clancy definitely likes attention."

I sip my beer. "So tell me something else. Tell me what food you like to eat."

He hesitates. "Italian. I like Japanese, too. And Mexican."

"That covers most of the culinary world," I say. "Now which do you prefer?"

"Pizza," he says with a smile. "You?"

"Ugh, I hate pizza. Pizza sucks. I don't know how anyone could like pizza."

"You...pizza? Really? Who hates pizza?"

I smile. "I have no idea. I love pizza."

He blows out a breath and laughs. "I like Van Halen. And Bon Jovi. And Cheap Trick."

"Love 'em," I say. "Eddie Van Halen is one of the greats."

"That's right," he says. "You must know a lot about music. You play guitar like your dad?"

"Yep. I met Eddie once. My dad was recording and Eddie walked in, and they started jamming. I wish I appreciated it more at the time."

"How old were you?" he asks.

"Six. I still have the recording. I should go back and listen to it."

"Is it out there? Are there other copies?"

"Not that I know of," I say.

Spencer shakes his head. "That would be worth some major bucks. You should keep it in a safe."

"Thanks, Mr. Lawyer," I say with a smile. "I have a question. Do you think fame is worth it? I mean, I don't want to be famous, but I want to play my music. Do you think it's worth it?"

He clears his throat. "Do you want my professional opinion, or my personal opinion?"

"They're different?" I ask.

He nods. "Professionally, I'd tell you that of course it's worth it. The big money comes with fame. But personally...no. It's not worth it."

"Why not?"

"We represent over 640 clients in the entertainment industry. I can name maybe five who aren't completely screwed up."

"Artists tend to be that way," I say. "The question is, were they screwed up to begin with, or did the fame screw them up?"

He slugs his beer. "Doesn't matter. Fame intensifies it. Fame contributes. Fame makes it harder to deal with personal issues. I wouldn't touch it with a ten-foot pole."

I sigh. "I think I knew that. I wish it weren't the case, but it is."

"Actually…you could pull a Hannah Montana. You watched that show as a kid, right?"

"That's a television show," I say. "Not reality. In real life, how could you possibly keep your identity a secret?"

"It can be done," he says. "You just don't see it done because entertainers are fame whores. It could totally be done."

I'll chew on that another time.

"Tell me something nobody knows about you," I say.

"Hmm. I write science fiction every night before I go to bed."

"Who's your favorite author?"

"J.S. Savage. You know him?"

I nod. "I'm a sci fi nerd. You like fantasy, too?"

"Duh. *World of Warcraft? Dungeons and Dragons?*"

"Ever played *7 Wonders?*"

Spencer laughs. "We have weekly tournaments. You should come some time."

"I'd love that."

We smile at each other. I like this guy.

Chet comes over to the table, a pout on his lips. "What are you two laughing about? Come back over and join us."

Spencer stands quickly and holds out a hand to me. I smile and take it.

❧

It's after eleven, and though I've had a great night, the three beers I've had are making me yawn. Chet notices and smiles at me.

"That's our cue," he says. "Shall we call it a night?"

Clancy frowns. "The night is young! Let's go bowling!"

Spencer looks at me, and I laugh. "Bowling? I haven't been bowling since the eighth grade."

"They have Rock 'N Bowl at the Newport Striker Lanes," Clancy says. "Loud music, neon lights, and fried mac and cheese balls. It'll be awesome."

Spencer smiles. "I'm up for it if you are."

"Do you actually want to go?" I ask.

He glances at the other two men and then looks back at me. "I'd like a little more time with you."

Ahhh.

So we head over for a little Rock 'N Bowl.

My first mistake is my choice of footwear: I have no socks. But for the low, low price of $8.00 (Spencer insists on handing me a $10 bill), I can get a little pair of low-cut socks, complete with a bouncy little ball at the back of the heel, out of a vending machine. They're all sold out of white, apparently, so I can choose lime green or hot pink. I go with the pink to match my sneaky bra strap.

I'm the last to get my shoes, since the dickhead behind the counter wouldn't give them to me until I proved I had socks. The boys have already changed, and it's freaking hilarious.

Clancy pulls the clown shoes off, but he's the most casual in jeans and a button-down paisley shirt. Chet looks like a rich janitor in his khakis and Polo. And poor Spencer. Size 14 shoes—in tricolored red, green, and white—don't go so well with a navy pin-stripe suit.

But as we all laugh together about the absurdity of our footwear…I take it back. Spencer with his square-frame glasses and his perfect crew cut and his larger-than-average-but-still-sexy nose and his meek manner and his sweet shyness…the shoes fit him perfectly.

"Choose a ball, love," Clancy says. "Aim for a ten-pounder."

I choose an orange-marbled ten-pound ball, and I almost drop it on my foot. Holy crap, is it heavy. So I hunt for a nine, but they don't seem to make them, and end up with an eight. My fingers stick a bit in the holes, but at least it's light.

I notice Chet picks a twelve-pound ball, Clancy a fourteen, and Spencer a sixteen. Yes, I'm impressed. That's two gallons of milk right there.

"Do you lift weights?" I ask him as Clancy puts our names into the computer. I have to lean in real close to his ear, since the music's so loud, and I give it a good look. It's totally clean, no hair or earwax or weird crust. Excellent.

"I swim every morning," he yells back into my ear. I pray I don't have any ear funk. "You?"

I just shake my head. My lack of daily exercise is about to become apparent.

"You're up first," Clancy mouths to me.

Of course.

Okay, so my upper body strength is shit. We know that. But I have nimble fingers and excellent wrist strength and control. If I can just get my arm to swing the weight of the ball, I should be able to aim it.

I stand at the line, everyone staring at me. I know this because I turn and give them a small smile before facing forward again. Right. Clancy gave me a little demonstration, and I just have to copy him. Two steps, swing, release. Right.

I take two steps…whoops! Forgot to swing. My feet slide on the slick waxed floor, and I do a little tap dance to get my footing.

"Sorry," I say. "Gonna try that again."

I go back to the line and take a deep breath. I don't bother looking back at the guys this time, 'cause they're probably all laughing at me.

I take one step, swing my arm back, take a second step, and that front foot just keeps on sliding. In my panic, I swing the ball forward, and my chubby fingers stick, seriously delaying the release of the ball. The weight of the ball finally pulls it from my fingers, and it sails above my head. I land in a perfect split, and I watch the ball crash with a loud thunk a foot in front of the line and roll slowly into the gutter.

I look back at the boys, who are all wide-eyed.

"At least I hit the right lane," I say.

⁋

Yes, I also ripped my jeans. The top button tore right off when I did those splits and pinged down the lane. I think it was the middle of the second game before Chet managed to hit the button with his ball and push it into the gutter.

Spencer was gracious enough to remove his jacket and drape it around my waist as he hoisted me to my feet. He even tied the arms in a neat knot for me. Which was chivalrous. My jeans were in no danger of sliding off, but they did gape at the top, showing off my hot pink thong. And that was not something I wanted the entire bowling alley to see.

Back at the bar, Spencer walks me to my car. Sparks aren't flying, but there is something there. He is such a nice guy. And after my father…I value nice.

"I had fun," I say. "Thanks for being my blind date."

He looks at the ground and awkwardly shuffles his face. "You had fun?"

"Yeah. Didn't you?"

He finally looks at me. "Of course. Yeah. I mean, yes. I had fun."

"But?"

He blows out a breath, and I watch him gather himself. "I…can I kiss you goodnight?"

Some women would find this a turnoff—I read enough romance novels to know this. But in my twenty-eight years, no one's ever asked me. And, also for the first time in my life, I like that I have a choice.

I put my hands on his chest and go up on tiptoe. He smiles, and I notice a dimple at the left corner of his mouth. His body is shaking under my hands, and I know how much it cost him to ask me. So I soften my lips and touch them to his, and he kisses me.

His lips are plump and soft. He puts his hands on my shoulders and squeezes tight, like he doesn't want to let go. It's such a small gesture, such an affectionate rather than sexual one, that it actually makes my heart skip a beat.

He pulls me into a hug and I nuzzle into his chest.

"Can I see you again?" he asks.

I look up at him and nod. "Call me."

"This is…I hope you don't think this is weird, but…would you text me when you get home? I just want to make sure you arrive safely."

Wow. "I think that's really sweet. Of course."

We say goodnight, and I drive back home. Before I even hang up my keys, I text Spencer that I'm home safe and sound.

He insists that I don't let the bed bugs bite.

Chapter 25

Sunday brunch with my mother. I tell her about my date with Spencer, and she's clearly not happy.

"You're a client, Hope," she says. "I don't like this. That firm knows a helluva lot about us. He can find out anything he wants to know."

"It's not like we have anything to hide," I say. "Once someone knows we own the rights to Dad's work, they can pretty much extrapolate our net worth."

She presses her lips together.

"Is there something else?" I ask. "Something you're not telling me?"

"I just want you to reconsider. Business and pleasure don't mix."

"It was one date," I say. "One kiss. It's not like we're getting married."

"I won't say another word," she says. "You know where I stand."

Actually, I don't. There are over a hundred lawyers at the firm, and Spencer doesn't even work in the music industry. My mother is making a mountain out of a molehill.

"So what's on tap next?" she asks. "On the hobby front."

I sigh. "Not bowling. That's for damn sure."

She smiles. "How about something quiet? Like knitting?"

"Funny you should say that. I've actually been thinking about knitting."

"Dear God," she says. "I was joking. Grandma Helen had a knitting addiction. When you were just a baby… that was the height of her mania. Our house was covered in yarn—tissue box cozies, tea kettle cozies, butt-ugly Christmas ornaments. The woman actually knitted a cover for a fly swatter. How gross is that?"

I laugh. "I have a purpose for the knitting. Martika's pregnant."

My mother grins. "Oh, how wonderful! A baby! Benny must be thrilled."

"He's more scared shitless right now, but I think we can get him to thrilled."

"It's settled, then," she says. "You have to knit. I still have the baby blanket Grandma knitted for you."

"You do? Where is it? I'd love to have it."

"You can have it when I'm dead," she says. "I sleep with it." I raise an eyebrow and she waves a hand. "Don't say a word. It's part of my therapy."

"And how long have you been sleeping with it?" I ask.

"Since…a while."

"Why?"

She lowers her eyes and straightens the napkin in her lap. "It's supposed to be a reminder. I wrapped you up in that blanket every night, and I washed it every day. I didn't do everything wrong."

I reach across the table and wiggle my fingers. She smiles and puts her hand in mine.

"You did a lot right," I say. "You're doing a lot right. Hell, I'm gonna bury you with that blanket."

She blows out a breath. "Thank God. I'd probably haunt you without it."

Chapter 26

Benny calls me as I'm driving home from work. "Hey, are you free tonight?"

"Yeah. What's up?"

"Martika's sick as a dog, and I just got called in to work. I was hoping you could sit with her."

I make a U-turn and head in their direction. "No problem. Can I get her anything? A smoothie, or some Pepto Bismol?"

"Let me ask her." I can hear him speaking to her in soothing tones. "Ice cream. Pistachio."

"On it. I'll be there soon."

It takes me about fifteen minutes to pick up the ice cream and get to their house. Poor Martika is doubled over on the couch, rocking back and forth, a small trashcan in her hands.

"It's morning sickness," Benny says, taking the ice cream from me and putting it in the freezer. "But apparently it should be called all-day sickness."

I smile at him. "Go. I've got her."

I sit next to her and rub her back. "I brought your ice cream."

"Sounds great," she says with a moan. "If I can just get past this bout…it will help." She closes her eyes and cradles the trashcan to her chest. "Oh, God."

She sucks her bottom lip into her mouth. I can see her fighting the nausea. And then she buries her head in the trashcan and heaves.

Oh, no. The smell…I'm not good with smells. I breathe through my mouth and keep rubbing her back.

She heaves again.

I gag. Shit! I can't lose it now.

She passes me the bucket and grabs a glass of water off the end table. She swishes the water in her mouth and spits it into the trashcan.

Poor girl. Snot is running from her nose, and her eyes are red and tear-filled.

"Let me get a tissue," I say. "Do you need the bucket?"

She shakes her head and curls into a ball.

Luckily, Ben has lined the trashcan. I take the bag out and twist it shut, leaving the can for Martika, just in case.

I gag again, and my mouth floods with saliva. No, no, no, I will not throw up!

I run through the house and to the side yard, dumping the bag. Then I run back to the bathroom and grab a box of tissues. Martika is again bent over the trashcan, spewing.

"What the hell have you been eating?" I ask.

"Don't make me laugh," she says, setting the can down and taking a few tissues from my hand. "Popcorn, extra butter. It sounded good at the time. I think I'm ready for ice cream."

I laugh. "Seriously? You just threw up like six times."

"Sugar," she says. "Sugar helps."

I'm doubtful, but hey, it's not my stomach.

I take the trashcan with me to the kitchen and rinse it out in the sink. Ugh. I try not to look, but my eye catches on the mess as it swirls down the drain. Several chunks of popcorn stick to the sides of the sink.

I gag again. And then I make the colossal mistake of taking a breath through my nose. Noxious vomit wafts to my nostrils, and I gag again. I put my hands on the edge of the counter and fight it.

"I'll just take it out of the carton," Martika calls. "Hurry."

Right.

I get the small container of Ben and Jerry's out of the freezer. I pry the lid off and grab a spoon, and my stomach rolls. Christ. I'm almost to the den when I gag yet again. I turn back to the kitchen…I can make it to the sink…run, feet, run!

But I'm not fast enough. I vomit all over Martika's Ben and Jerry's.

Chapter 27

Saturday night at Spencer's for a *7 Wonders* showdown. Right on. I haven't played the game since the divorce—it was one of Matt's favorites—but I know what I'm doing.

I am the only girl, which isn't surprising. What is surprising is that all five of these guys are lawyers, all over the age of thirty-five. You'd think they'd have something more important to do.

Not that I'm judging. I could play this game all night.

"So what's your strategy?" Spencer asks as our cards are dealt.

"I go where my cards take me," I say. "You?"

He grins. "Same. But most of these guys have one way they like to win. Watch for it."

I nod.

This is a little hard-core for me. Apparently, there's no talking during the game. The first time I try to ask IP Attorney Steve to my left about his job, I get shushed. With an actual finger to my lips.

"Don't take it personally," Real Estate Attorney Taylor says. "We had to institute a no-talking rule since the great Cheating Scandal of 2013."

"I guess I'll ask about that after the game," I say, and they all laugh. And then they shut up.

As the points are being tallied at the end of the first game, Spencer gets a call. He wanders into the kitchen.

"So the cheating scandal," I say. "Sounds scandalous."

Steve laughs. "Alan and I decided we'd form a secret alliance. We had code words for the cards we wanted, hand signals for what was going down."

"And you got caught," I say. "Smooth. Who's Alan?"

"He works with Spencer," Steve says. "Couldn't get a babysitter, or he'd be here."

"I'm gonna grab a beer," I say, standing. "Anyone want anything?"

Spencer comes back in with a bottle of whiskey and a tray of high-ball glasses, his phone wedged between his shoulder and his ear. "I filed it," he says. "Fuck that. Send Dan…yes, I got a confirmation. Are you freaking kidding me?"

He sets down the bottle and slides the tray on the table. The phone falls to his hand.

"I have to bail," he says. "My fucking secretary didn't …whatever. I don't have the energy to explain. I have to run to the office."

"Dude, come on!" Steve says. "Fuck 'em. You can go in the morning."

"Can't," he says. "I shouldn't be long. An hour at most."

"But we were gonna do teams this round!" Steve cries, as though all his plans have gone to hell.

"When I get back. Hope?" Spencer nods his head to the kitchen, and I follow him in. "I'm sorry about this. I truly won't be long. Will you be okay here?"

I smile. "I'm fine. Do what you need to do. An hour's not that long."

"It would be if you were the one leaving," he says.

I blush.

He kisses my cheek, and out he goes.

The guys have poured the whiskey neat, and they're all in the process of lighting cigars.

"You want one?" Steve asks.

I hesitate. "I've never smoked."

"It's not like smoking a cigarette. You just puff on it. For the taste."

He shows me how to cut off the end and how to get it lit. I try not to inhale, but the smoke hits the back of my throat, and I cough hard, my cheeks going red and my eyes tearing.

Steve pats my back while he laughs. "I told you not to inhale."

"Right," I say. Cough, cough. I take a sip of whiskey to try to soothe the burn, but the whiskey burns more, and I double over with a coughing fit.

Everyone's laughing at me.

And suddenly the front door opens. "I'm here. Let the par-tay begin!"

"Alan," Steve says to me. He pops to his feet and shakes the guy's hand. "My partner in crime."

"Jessica got home early from her movie," he says. "I figured it was early enough to make an appearance." He notices me sitting here, puffing on my cigar. "And who is this?"

I shift the cigar to my left hand and stand. "Hope. I'm friends with Spencer. Nice to meet you."

"Likewise," he says, holding my hand too long. "I didn't know Spencer had such beautiful friends."

I raise an eyebrow. "You're married and you're hitting on me?"

"Divorced," he says. "I'm not that big a douchebag."

"And why are you divorced?"

Alan laughs. "Okay, so I am a douchebag. Pour me a whiskey, my friend."

Steve hands him Spencer's glass, and Alan takes Spencer's chair to my right and drinks deep.

"So Spencer, huh?"

"We just met a week ago, but he's nice. I like him."

Alan shakes his head. "No accounting for taste."

I look around the table. Taylor and Michael and meek little Stan are all doing statue impressions.

"Why would you talk about a friend and colleague that way?" I ask.

Alan smiles. "I was only joking. Lighten up, babe."

Babe?

I'm not sure what to do. I mean, I know what I want to do, but I don't want to leave when Spencer expects me to be here. I grit my teeth and promise to tell Alan the Asshole off at the end of the night.

"You close that deal?" Steve asks him.

He holds up two fingers. "Two, baby. Two deals this week on my biggest account. I'm putting a deposit on that new Jaguar tomorrow."

"So the old biddy agreed to sign," Steve says. "Took her long enough."

Alan lights his cigar and waves the match out. "I take my fiduciary responsibility to my clients very seriously. Very seriously."

Taylor sits back in his chair. "You mean the Spotify deal? That's the one you closed?"

"And the Horton campaign," he says, nodding. "Fucking three million dollars to play those songs at his rallies for the next three months, and there's still over a year to go until the election. Easy money, bro."

"Senator Horton paid three million dollars to use some songs at his rallies?" I say. "Whose songs?"

"Joe Cruz," he says. "Fucking tightwad estate doesn't make half of what it could. They have 'principles,'" he says, giving me air quotes.

My heart sinks to my feet, and my body starts to shake.

I knock back my whiskey and lick my lips. "Joe Cruz?"

Alan smiles. "Amazing, isn't it? You can't even get his songs on iTunes yet."

"Joe Cruz…really?" My mouth can't seem to form the words I want to say.

He pats my arm and laughs. "You must be a fan. Hey, I'll talk to the estate for you. I'm sure I can sweet-talk them into sending me a few t-shirts or something." He smiles wide at the whole table, like he's the fucking Joe Cruz superhero.

"Who…" I start to say, and then I have to clear my throat. "Who gave you permission to let Horton use those songs?"

Alan looks at me, and I lower my eyes. "What's it to you?"

"Joe…Joe Cruz is…" And then I lift my head and hold his gaze. "I'm the fucking tightwad estate."

He blinks. And then he laughs. "Yeah, right."

"I'm Hope Cruz. I want you to get...I want you to get your ass on the phone and call the Horton campaign right now. If they play even one second of one my father's songs, I'm gonna sue that fucking smile off your face."

He sets his whiskey down and plucks the cigar from his mouth. "Hey, now. Take it easy. You're Hope Cruz?"

"I meant what I said. You have thirty seconds to get on the phone."

"Your mother, she's the one I always deal with. She—"

"Would never have agreed to this," I say. "Never. And I know you need both of our signatures anyway."

Alan looks at Steve, who's frozen in place.

"Think about it for a second," Alan says. "This isn't chump change. You can make millions of dollars. Horton—"

"Senator Horton wants to legalize drugs. All drugs. I won't support that, no matter how much money it makes me, because drugs ruined my father's life. You want to laugh at my principles, go right ahead. I'll take my business elsewhere."

"You can't—"

"I can," I say, pushing to my feet. "And I'll be sure to let the managing partner know my reasons for leaving."

He stands up beside me and tries to take my arm, but I shrug him off. "Just calm down," he says. "Sit back down and let's talk about this."

I fold my arms over my chest. "Did you get my mother's permission to do this?"

"I'm a fucking great attorney," he says. "I have always looked out for your best interest."

"Answer my question."

He just stares at me until it becomes too much, and then he looks away.

"As of tonight, you're fired," I say. "I'll be sending someone to conduct a full accounting of my interests. And for the record, you were right. You are a douchebag."

∞

I almost drive straight to my mother's house, but it's after ten. She's likely asleep.

And I can't possibly sleep. I spend an hour gathering all my statements from Mayberry, all my emails, all my contracts. I'm hiring a forensic accountant first thing in the morning.

My doorbell rings. Spencer.

"Hey," he says. "Chet told me where you live."

"You could have asked me," I say.

He shrugs. "I wasn't sure you'd take my call."

I wave him in and we sit on the couch.

"Why wouldn't I take your call? You didn't do anything wrong...did you?"

He sits back. "First, I knew Alan worked on your account, but I would never have asked him about it, AND...I only invited you 'cause I knew he wouldn't be there. I had no idea he'd show up."

I nod.

"And second...I didn't work on it, exactly, but Alan did ask me to look over a contract for your estate. About a year ago."

I frown. "Why would he ask you?"

"That *Cop Killer Reloaded* deal," he says. "We also look over the video game rights."

"What?" I shriek. "You're telling me that my dad's songs are being used in that disgusting video game?"

Spencer pales. "You didn't know?"

"Of course I didn't know!" I yell. "There's no fucking way I would profit off that! No fucking way!"

He scrubs a hand through his hair and stands, pulling out his phone. "I have to call some people," he says. "I won't let Alan get away this."

"I appreciate it," I say, "but I'll handle it. You have your job to think about."

"That's why I have to report it," he says. "I can't go down with the ship."

I nod.

"Hope…I'm so sorry. Not all attorneys are like Alan."

I nod again. "I think you should go."

He sags.

I put my arms around him in a hug. "You've been great. But I need to separate myself. Completely."

This time he nods. He kisses my cheek, and I show him out.

I lean back against the closed door and sigh.

Goodbye, Man #3.

Chapter 28

I get a phone call at one AM. I flop my arm to my nightstand, fumbling for the phone.

"Yeah what?" I mumble.

"Hey, it's Matt. Can you answer the door?"

I shove the hair out of my eyes and sit up. "You're at my door?"

"Yeah. Can you hurry? It's an emergency."

I slide my feet into some slippers and make my way to the door. "Come on!" I hear him yell.

I yank open the door and give him a glare. Matt's on my stoop with a leash in his hand, a puppy on the end of it.

"My parents' house is on fire," he says, shoving the leash in my hand. "I gotta go. Can you watch her?"

"I, uh, what? On fire?"

"I just got the call ten minutes ago. Here's some food, get her a bowl of water, take her out to pee. I'll be back as soon as I can."

"What's her name?"

"It doesn't matter—"

"I can't just call her 'Hey You.'"

He blows out a breath. "Strings."

"Strings."

"Gotta go. I'll call you."

"Don't," I say. "Just come by after ten. We'll be fine."

"Thank you." And he rushes off.

Strings. Holy crap.

He named his dog after me.

And holy, holy crap. His parents' house is on fire!

☙

Strings is the cutest little thing I've ever seen. She's a chocolate lab with light blue eyes, so small she fits in my lap. I remove the leash and carry her to the kitchen, where I fill one bowl with water and the other with food. And that is my extent of dog care-taking knowledge. I've never had a pet.

Not to mention the fact that I'm butt-ass tired.

Maybe she can sleep with me. Since it's the middle of the night, she must be tired, too.

I set her in the middle of the comforter and crawl under the covers. She bounds over to me and licks my face.

"Whoa, dog," I say. "Sleep. It's time for sleep. Not play."

I put her two feet away and lie back down.

The dog gets back up and starts nipping at my hand.

Maybe she wants to be petted.

So I pat the top of her head. "There you go. Sleep."

But she wiggles under my hand and pops to her feet. I don't really know how she's standing, as the comforter is so plush it engulfs her.

Then she yips. She bounds over to me, nips and tugs at my hair, and then bounds away as I rise. She leans forward and wags her tongue, giving me a series of annoying little yips.

"I will not play," I say. "I'm going to sleep. I suggest you do the same."

I turn over and give her my back, snuggling into my pillow.

And then she's on me again, crawling over my shoulder, her rear feet scrambling at my back, until she spills over to my face, my nose buried in her puppy butt.

This clearly isn't going to work.

I get up and close the doors to my bathroom and closet. Now she's locked in. I set her on the floor and climb back into bed.

As far as I know, she doesn't bark again.

∞

I wake and stretch and glance at my clock. It's only seven on a Sunday morning, but I need to get up. Alan the Fucking Great Attorney is going down.

As I rise, a putrid scent reaches my nose. I grimace. Dear God, what is that? Did my toilet back up?

I put a bare foot on the wood floor, but the floor's all wet. Oh no! I have a sewer leak in my house!

I reach for the lamp on my nightstand and twist on the light.

My room looks like a bomb went off.

The three decorative pillows I keep on my bed have been torn to shreds, bits of cotton stuffing and goosedown feathers strewn about. My slippers have been chewed beyond all recognition. The braided rug at the foot of my bed is decidedly unbraided and has been...befouled.

Strings.

"Where are you?" I say. I step carefully, watching for any more pee or poop. "Come out here. You've been a naughty dog."

I hear a very faint, raspy cough of a bark. I follow the noise to the window. Strings is tangled in the curtains, lying on her side.

I pick her up. "Come on, you. You just cost me a lot of money, you know that?"

I carry her out to the kitchen, and then I look at her. She's limp, and her breathing is wheezy and labored.

"Oh my God, something's wrong with you. What's wrong?"

As if the dog will give me an answer.

And then she spasms, her eyes rolling back in her head. I cry out and run back to my room, cradling her to my chest.

"Hold on, hold on, hold on!" I yell, shoving my feet into my tennis shoes. I grab my purse and keys on the way out and race to my car.

⁊

I just keep her in my lap. She's breathing, but she's working way too hard at it.

I search for emergency vets on my phone and find one five miles away. Five miles sounds close. At least it did, until I start driving.

"Hang on, sweetie, hang on," I croon as I drive. Strings gags, and vomit leaks out the side of her mouth and drips down my leg. Tears pool in my eyes and drip down my cheeks. I can barely see to drive.

I blow through a red light. I roll down my window and wave one hand out.

"Emergency!" I yell. "Outta my way! Get the fuck outta my way!"

As soon as I have the building in sight, I'm yelling.

"Help! Help! Help me! Someone help me!"

I park the car and gather Strings to my chest. I run inside, yelling all the way.

"Help! She can't breathe! Help!"

A woman rushes over to me and takes Strings. "What happened?"

"Don't know," I say, as I follow her to a back room. "I woke up this morning and she was like this."

She places Strings on a table and bends over her. "I think there's something in her throat. Did she eat something she shouldn't have?"

I'm just staring at poor Strings. Why isn't the lady doing something? Why won't she MOVE?

A different woman comes over and takes my arm.

"Your dog will be fine," she says, leading me out of the room. I look back, trying not to take my eyes off the puppy. "How about a cup of coffee?"

I nod. She physically places me in a chair, and I put my head in my hands and sob.

She brings me a styrofoam cup of coffee and sits and rubs my back.

"How long have you had her?"

I lift my head. "What?"

"What's her name? How long have you had her?"

"Oh, she…she's not mine. A friend's. A friend had an emergency in the middle of the night, and I was supposed to be watching her. I was supposed to take care of her. It's all my fault."

"It's not your fault," she says firmly. "Accidents happen." She shoves the coffee into my hands and wraps my fingers around it. "Let me go see how she's doing, and then we can tackle the paperwork."

I stand. "Can I be with her?"

"Let me see what's going on first. Just rest."

I sink back into the chair and notice the coffee in my hands. I take a deep sip, but for the first time in my life, coffee doesn't make me feel better.

Fifteen minutes later, my tears are still flowing when the lady comes back out.

"We've got the x-rays," she says. "She had some fluff in her throat, which we removed fairly easily, so she's breathing now, but...she managed to eat something, and we're going to have to do surgery."

"Surgery?" I whisper. "Oh, God, no. No!"

She puts a hand on my shoulder. "It's routine, at least in our line of work. We're getting the bloodwork done now, and we're prepping for surgery. We just need your consent."

I squeeze my eyes shut. This means I have to call Matt.

"She has to live," I say. "You have to save her. Do whatever you need to do."

"I'll print out the forms and you can sign them," she says. She goes back behind the long counter and sits at a computer.

Christ. I pat my sides, searching for my phone. But not only don't I have a phone…I have no pockets. I look down at myself. I'm wearing a see-through white tank top, no bra…and a black pair of boy-shorts underwear.

"Be right back," I say, and I rush out to my car, but I realize I don't have my keys. But the door's open, wide open, my keys dangling from the ignition, my purse in plain sight on the passenger seat.

"Thank you, God," I say as I grab my keys and purse. I go to the back and pull open the lift. All I have is an Angels blanket that Matt and I used to take to night games, but it will do. I wrap it around myself and go back inside.

The lady has everything ready for me on a clipboard.

"Do you need the owner's permission?" I ask.

"Yours is fine," she says, "as long as you agree to financial responsibility."

"Financial?"

She points to an accounting at the bottom of the first page. The total is just over $3,000.

"The costs could change," she says. "It depends on how things go. But we're usually pretty accurate."

I don't blink. She goes through each paper with me, and I sign them all and pray.

"You go home now," the lady, Colleen is her name, says. "It'll probably be the afternoon before she's out of surgery."

"Go home? How can I go home? Won't she need me?"

Colleen gives me a hug. "Strings will be fine. She's in good hands. I'll call you as soon as you can see her."

I sniffle. "You promise?"

She smiles. "I promise."

ᔓ

So I wander back out to my car, wrapping the blanket tight around me, and I say a small prayer for myself. I think I'm going to need it.

I take a deep breath and dial Matt's number.

"Hey," he says, voice groggy. My eyes tear again. That's his sexy morning voice. "Did I oversleep?"

"No," I say. "Are your parents okay?"

I hear him shift around on his bed. "Yeah. Lost the kitchen, but the rest of the house is okay, barring some smoke and water damage."

"I'm so sorry," I say. "How awful."

"Gotta hand it to their insurance company, though," he says. "An adjuster showed up while the firemen were still there. He got them into a hotel."

"So you were saved by the insurance adjuster," I say, and he laughs.

"Yeah. Close one. How's…my dog?"

And then I burst into tears.

"Hey. What's wrong?"

"I almost killed her!" I wail.

"What?"

"She…I woke up this…sniff, sniff, morning, and she…she wasn't breathing right, so I took her to the vet, and she swallowed something. She's…having surgery."

I hear the bed squeak. "Where are you? I'm coming to you."

"I'm on my…my way home," I say, my voice laced with mucous. "Meet me there."

"Give me fifteen." And he hangs up.

I'm fucked.

Chapter 29

I was hoping to beat Matt home so I could change clothes, but that fucking five miles...

He's sitting on my front steps when I pull into the driveway. He has circles under his eyes, and the smile lines at the corners of his mouth look deeper than I remember them.

He jogs over to me as I get out. "We can take your car," he says, but I shake my head.

"I need to change. And they said she won't be awake until this afternoon. We can't see her now anyway."

"Shit," he says. "Have any beer?"

"You want a beer at nine o'clock in the morning?"

"I've only slept for two hours," he says. "It was more like a nap. We can say we're still partying."

I shake my head and open the front door. I throw the blanket on the back of the couch without thinking and head to the kitchen. I poke my head in the fridge and pull out a Corona. I pop the top and hold it out to him.

Matt is staring at me with an odd look on his face.

"Did you leave the house like that?"

"Like what?"

"Half naked?"

I look down at myself. Hell. I fold my arms over my chest. "It was an emergency."

"Tell me what happened."

"Follow me," I say. "I need some sweats."

We head to the bedroom, and the scent hits us both.

"Did you forget to take her out?" he asks.

"I…"

We reach my room and we both pause. The destruction is mind-blowing.

"I'm so sorry, Hope," Matt says. He bends down and picks something up. "I think this is a goner."

My red lace thong, chewed, is dangling from his finger. I snatch it quickly and scrunch it in my fist.

He leans forward and puts his hands on his knees. "Jesus Christ, I had no idea one puppy could do so much damage. I keep her in a cage at home."

I don't know what to say. The magnitude of the mess is just starting to hit me. My eyes sting, again, and I just concentrate on breathing.

"I'll clean up," he says. "Make yourself some coffee, and I'll clean up."

"I'll help," I say. "I already had coffee at the vet's."

"Then sit on the bed and tell me what happened. I need some cleaning stuff. At least you don't have carpet."

I get Matt the supplies he needs, pull on some sweats, then I sit on the bed and tell him what happened.

"Don't cry," he says. "It's my fault. I dumped her on you."

"About that," I say. "Why me?"

He pauses in his work. "Honestly? You're the only one I knew for sure would say yes."

I scowl at that. Some people would take it as a compliment, but not me. It only means I'm a doormat.

He finally stands and stretches. "So it looks like I'm on the hook for three or four pillows, your black flip-flops, a pair of slippers, one red lace thong, a rug, and new curtains. Anything I've missed?"

I shake my head.

"I can buy the stuff," he says. "Or would you rather do it and give me the bill?"

"I'm not letting you buy me underwear," I say. "And how would you even know what shoes to buy?"

"You're a size nine," he says. "I know your style. I could buy you shoes."

I blink. Now that I think about it, he probably could.

"I'll do it," I say.

"So…you hungry? I'll buy you breakfast." He turns to go, as though asking me is an automatic yes.

I stand up. "I don't think that's a good idea."

He turns back to me, a quizzical look on his face. "Come on. You've gotta be starving."

"I'm fine," I say. "As soon as I hear from the vet, I'll call you."

He takes a step back. "Are you sure?"

"I'm sure."

"Okay." And Matt walks out.

Chapter 30

I know I need to deal with legal stuff, but all I can think about is the puppy I almost murdered. I tell myself that no one's really at the firm on Sunday anyway, and I give myself permission to wallow.

And something else hinky is going on. Matt named his dog after me, and then he turned to me in a moment of crisis. What the hell is that about? Could he...might he actually regret leaving me?

I shut down that line of thinking. Whatever he's up to...it doesn't matter. I've moved on. Done.

When the call from the vet comes, I find I've fallen asleep on the couch. I take the time to brush my teeth and wash my face before I call Matt.

"She's out of surgery," I say. "She's gonna make it."

"Thank God," he says. "I'll pick you up and we'll go see her."

"See you soon."

Matt is silent on the drive to the vet's. I can't read him. Is he mad at me? Just worried? Tired? Who knows. I suddenly realize that I've never been able to read him. He's always hidden his feelings from me. It's a depressing thought.

Sweet little mess-maker Strings is awake but sleepy. Matt immediately puts his face to hers and gets a few licks. He cuddles her small head and scratches behind her ears and whispers to her.

It's the sweetest thing I've ever seen. I mean, I've seen him with dogs. His parents have always had a couple. He grew up with him. I knew he was good with dogs.

Out of sight, out of mind, for me. I never considered us getting a dog. And he never asked. I wonder why. He knows I would have agreed. I always agreed.

Matt straightens and turns to me. "You wanna?" he waves at Strings.

So I walk over and put my face to hers. She nuzzles my nose with hers and gives me a lick. I laugh.

"Thank God you're okay," I say, rubbing my cheek to hers. "You're a little fighter, you are."

The vet comes in and shakes our hands. "We'd like to keep her for a couple of days," she says. "She's fine, but she's still young, and I want to keep an eye on her."

Impulsively, I throw my arms around the doctor. "Thank you," I whisper. "Thank you so so much."

She smiles and pats my back.

She explains the post-op procedures and caregiving, and we each give Strings a little more love.

"Oh," Matt says. "You didn't say what she ate."

The doctor looks at me. "Oh, I…it was tough to tell what it was."

"You don't have any idea?"

Then she laughs. "Fine. It was part of a…a tampon."

છ

"I won't ask where the hell she found a tampon," Matt says as we slide into his Jeep. "With everything she chewed, it could have been half a dozen things."

I just…don't know what to say. It had to come from the pocket of my jeans on the floor. I'm expecting my period to start any minute, and I wanted to be prepared last night. But it's no business of Matt's.

"You surprised me," he says.

"How's that?"

"I've never seen you like that. Nurturing."

"I'm nurturing."

He shakes his head. "I didn't mean it like that. You are. I just…this was different."

"How?" I say.

"You…I could never picture us having kids," he says. "I know we talked about it and stuff, but I could never really picture you as a mother.

Andrea Ring

And today…I could totally see it. I've just never experienced that side of you."

Again, I'm at a loss for words. I've never acted like a mother because I've never had the chance. I've never had a pet, never been around children…of course I've never acted like a mother. I've never BEEN a mother!

Matt pulls into the driveway and I put my hand on the door handle.

"Wait," he says. "Wait." So I turn to him. "I…thank you for taking care of Strings. You saved her life."

I nod.

"And…maybe I can come inside."

"Why?"

He blows out a breath. "Jesus, Hope, work with me here. You fucking turned me on."

"I…what?"

He shuts off the ignition and shifts to me. "You're different. You're really working on yourself, and I can see it. You turned me down for breakfast, and you loved my dog…" And he leans forward.

I stare into his eyes. Matt has the kindest eyes. My breathing speeds, and I take a deep breath, and I can smell, faintly, his coconut shampoo, and I watch his throat work, and my hands itch. They want to touch him.

I lean into him, but stop just a heartbeat out of reach.

"Hope," he whispers. "I've fucking missed you."

"I've…"

I almost say it back. *I've missed you, too, Matt.*

Except in the past three months…I haven't.

I pull away. "I'm sorry. I have to go."

And I exit the car and head inside.

To Be Continued…

BOOKS BY ANDREA RING

Stand-Alone Contemporary Romance

High Maintenance

Young Adult Contemporary Romance

A Yellow Wood Series

Under Water (Book 1)

Breaking the Surface (Book 2)

Romantic Fantasy

Nilaruna Cycles

The Go-Between (Book 1)

The Princess (Book 2)

Goddess (Book 3)

Science Fiction

The System Series

Nervous System (Book 1)

Systematic (Book 2)

Operating System (Book 3)

Honor System (Book 4)

Systems Go (Book 5)

Note to my readers: I'm humbled and grateful that you read my work. I hope it touched you. Send me an email. Write a review on Amazon. Comment on my blog. You're the reason I write, and I'll never forget that.

Read a chapter from the next episode in The String Serial,

Second String

The String Serial
Part Two

I call in sick to work and drive to my mother's. She's sipping coffee in her yoga pants, gearing up for an early-morning class.

"Did you get fired?" she asks as she pecks my cheek and moves to the kitchen.

"Why would you think I got fired?"

She pours me a cup of coffee. "It's a Monday morning and you're supposed to be at work. Was there a gas leak?"

I sigh and sip my coffee. "I called in sick. We have a huge problem with Mayberry & Foster." My mother gives me a blank stare. "Mayberry & Foster. The firm that handles Dad's music rights?"

"Oh." She goes back to her place on the couch, and I follow her. "What problem is that?"

"Did you agree to let Dad's songs be used in that video game?"

"We signed to that hero game. The one where you play along with the fake guitar with those rainbow buttons."

"Not that one," I say. "It's called *Cop Killer Reloaded*."

"*Cop Killer*?" she says with a grimace. "That game is sick. No."

"What about Senator Horton's campaign? Did you know about that?"

She swallows her coffee. "You can't get worked up about all these inquires, Hope. Our attorneys bring us the deals, and we agree or not.

It's not Mayberry's fault some jackass wants the songs."

"I'm not worked up about inquires," I say. "So they brought the Horton thing to you. And you turned them down?"

"Of course I did," she says. "Don't tell me you think we should do it."

I shake my head. "It's done. I ran into one of our attorneys last night, and he didn't know who I was. He let it slip that he closed both the Spotify deal and the Horton campaign deal for us. And Dad's songs have been in that *Cop Killer* game for a year."

She pales. "That's not possible. And you and I discussed the subscription service deals, and we decided against them. I had a very pointed conversation with them about it."

"Is it possible you signed something you shouldn't have?" I ask. "I mean, I don't know how they expect to get away with this. These are three very visible deals. They couldn't expect to hide them from us forever."

"It's possible," she finally admits. "I never signed your name, though. I wouldn't do that."

I rise. "I need to hire a new attorney, just for this. And then we need someone else to represent Dad's catalog."

"I can't believe this," she says. "These are attorneys! They're supposed to follow the law."

I just laugh. "Ironic, isn't it?"

About the Author

Andrea Ring was born and raised in Orange County, California. At age eight, she wrote an essay proclaiming she wanted to be an "auther" when she grew up. It only took her thirty years to realize her dream.

She enjoys beating her four children at Boggle, reading science fiction and fantasy, and eating bacon. She hates to exercise, but loves taking walks with her family through Old Towne Orange. She's lucky to be married to the love of her life.

She thinks every book should contain a love story.

Did we mention her love of bacon?